JEFF JACKSON'S

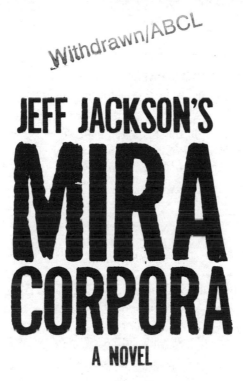

MIRA CORPORA

A NOVEL

TWO DOLLAR RADIO
Books too loud to ignore.

TWO DOLLAR RADIO is a family-run outfit founded in 2005 with the mission to reaffirm the cultural and artistic spirit of the publishing industry.

We aim to do this by presenting bold works of literary merit, each book, individually and collectively, providing a sonic progression that we believe to be too loud to ignore.

For Stephanie

Eternal thanks: Alethea Black, Giorgio Hiatt, Anna Stein, and John McElwee.

Artwork: Michael Salerno
Image of crown: *Graffiti Skull*, Matt Francis, July 5, 2009; www.flickr.com/photos/mattfrancis/3732877231

Typeset in Garamond, the best font ever.
Printed in the United States of America.

TWO DOLLAR RADIO
Books too loud to ignore.
www.TwoDollarRadio.com
twodollar@TwoDollarRadio.com

AUTHOR'S NOTE

This novel is based on the journals I kept growing up. When I rediscovered these documents, they helped me confront the fragments of my childhood and understand that the gaps are also part of the whole. Sometimes it's been difficult to tell my memories from my fantasies, but that was true even then. Throughout I've tried to honor the source material and my early attempts to wrest these experiences into language.

CONTENTS

"There is another world, but it is in this one."
—Paul Éluard

MIRA
CORPORA

I BEGIN

There's an empty notebook in the bottom drawer of my desk. I place it on a flat surface. I fold it open to the third page. I tap my pen against the paper three times. Then I draw the picture of a door and beneath it write the word "open."

The floor beneath me begins to shift. I keep my eyes fixed on the page, where the door is now ajar to reveal a staircase. I enter the page and walk down the steps. In pitch dark, I feel the way with my hands, running my fingertips along the walls. I move slow and breathe deep.

There is a bottom and my feet experience the relief of flat ground. I stand still and let my eyes adjust. A pinpoint of light beckons in the distance. I follow its faint glow as I move down the corridor. Soon I enter a round room with no windows. Torches encircle the rough stone walls. A wooden altar stands at the center of the space.

I look closer. A boy with alabaster skin—always alabaster— is tied to the altar with twine. He's bare except for a modest loin-cloth and I can see the blue veins beneath his pale skin. A delicate specimen. His body briefly spasms in a struggle against his bonds, but it's just a twinge of animal instinct without much conviction.

I'm careful to prepare this sacrament correctly. I start by plucking the stray hairs from the boy's otherwise smooth chest. Soon his skin appears as blank as a page. A steel dagger lies next to the body. I grip it tightly. As I approach the empty surface, the blade feels as sharp as a quill. I'm ready to begin.

CHAPTER 1
MY YEAR ZERO
(6 years old)

"We never have to stretch our imaginations,
it is our own lives we can't believe."
–The Mekons

THEY TAKE ME OUT HUNTING FOR STRAYS. PEOPLE stride through the woods and shout things at one another. They practice propping guns on their shoulders and breaking them in half so the empty shells tumble to the ground. Everybody here is older than me. I'm small and constantly underfoot. It's the afternoon, or something like that. Sunlight breaks through the trees to illuminate kaleidoscopic patterns on the forest floor. Pine needles, fallen leaves, patches of dirt. The pack of stray dogs barks in the distance. These are the first things I remember. Gunshots. Popping sounds. Little bursts of gray powder blooming from the end of each rifle.

Of course there are things before the first things: A stone farm-house, warm meals served on white plates, a large room filled with narrow beds tucked with wool blankets. But this hunt is my beginning. The kids fanning through the forest. The slow-motion ballet of soundless steps. The silent chorus of raised rifles.

A bearded man orders all the children to circle up and divide into groups. A brother and sister pair pull my ears and claim me. "We want Jeff," they chant. They say I'm their lucky charm. The siblings are both pale with spindly legs, denim shorts, floppy hiking boots. We set off into the heart of the woods. The boy's crew cut ends in a braided rat's tail. He flicks it back and forth across his shoulders. They both have beady eyes and big noses. There's something else on their faces, but it's not clear yet.

The boy hisses at me to keep up. My short and pudgy legs are sore, but I'm determined not to complain. There's a chill from the intense shade of the forest. A trickle of snot tickles my upper lip. A pebble bounces around inside my shoe. When I break into a trot, I stumble on a tree root and fall. There's something wet on my palms. Maybe it's blood, or possibly only reddish mud. I can't quite remember. The girl grabs my hand and tugs. She says: "Faster."

An adult blows a whistle and the hunting parties halt at the blacktop road. We cross the highway together and pause in a clearing. Everyone stands so still that horseflies start to land on us. I see it now: Everyone wears masks on their faces. Black masks with sequins. White masks with feathers. Red masks with long crooked noses. Even I'm wearing a mask. Several of the adults crouch by a patch of raw dirt to examine the fresh claw marks left by the pack of dogs. You can hear the faint echo of harried yelps and shivering leaves as the animals hurtle through the bushes.

The dogs bark more loudly in the distance. The siblings have loaded me down with a heavy backpack. The nylon straps dig into my small shoulders. There's a canteen in the outer pouch and the water tastes like cold metal. The siblings remain silent and converse by shifting the whites of their eyes. They seem to be intently following some unmarked trail. The boy scouts ahead and marks the path with spit.

The other groups are nowhere to be seen, but the electricity of the hunt surges around us. Bristling undergrowth. Rattled birdsong. Nearby gunshots. The boy and girl both throw their masks into the bushes. I follow their lead. We stop and listen to a series of high-pitched whines. My throat tightens. I know it's the sound of a stray dying without knowing how I know. It's a terrible sound. The siblings clutch their guns tighter. They'll go off in a minute, but not yet.

We rest by a tree stump. The girl removes a pack of cigarettes from her denim shorts and the siblings each light up. "We're not bad at hunting," the girl says to me. "We've just got a different plan." They pull the smoke into their mouths then exhale, over and over. Their faces seem ancient. The boy makes perfect smoke rings. I pucker my lips and pretend to blow circles in mute admiration. Maybe they've brought me along to teach me something. They whisper.

We stand in a clearing with a small tree. The girl kneels ceremoniously on the grass and unzips the inner pouch of the backpack. The boy instructs me to sit against a tree. The siblings shake some rope from the bag and wrap it tightly around the slender trunk. I mean, they wrap the rope tightly around me. They remove some glass jars from the pack and unscrew the aluminum lids. They smear my entire body with runny chunks of dog food and slimy kitchen grease. Some of the gritty brown paste sticks in my eyes and I blink it away. There's a word they each keep using. The boy pronounces it with a slight stammer. He says: "B-bait."

Even now I can still smell it: a foul stench, like overly spiced meat that binds me firmly to the clearing. The boy and girl shoot at the trees and watch the frenzied birds scatter into the far corners of the sky. They're waiting for the dogs to arrive. Insects crawl onto my hands and swarm my knees. Ants, mostly. Once a butterfly lands on my elbow, purple wings still as its body twitches. It seems to be stuck in the tacky paste, its tiny feet frantically pumping up and down. I can almost feel its heart screaming.

I can't stop coughing. My throat gags. I won't let myself cry. The wind has fallen dead and the metallic chirp of the insects accompanies the siblings as they submerge themselves in the bushes at the rim of the clearing. The round black holes of their guns flit between the green leaves like a pair of watchful eyes.

I have no idea where the siblings have gone. I call for help, but there's no reply. I can't even remember when they left. I'm having trouble keeping up with what's happening. The streaks of food have hardened and it feels like I'm trapped inside a thin shell. The sky turns the color of a peeled orange. The falling shadows start to obscure my sightlines. The edges of the woods vanish into nothingness.

The night is populated with shining green eyes. The pack of stray dogs surrounds me. They sniff the air and growl. Twitching noses, bristling whiskers. I remain perfectly still. When one of them bares its yellow teeth, I start to wail. A wet warmth spreads through my pants. They circle closer. There aren't so many of them. Their movements are tentative and hobbled. Their thick brown coats are matted with tufts of dried blood. I'm surprised to find their faces are kind. We gaze into each other's eyes. They begin to lick my face with their rough tongues.

The ropes I've been tied with are slippery. Maybe they've been this way all along. I wriggle loose from the tree, arch my back, and stretch my body. The clearing is empty. The moon is bright overhead. Bits of its light are mirrored in the shiny surfaces of the leaves. A fresh breeze combs through my hair and clothes. I feel strangely happy.

I walk in a perfectly straight line through the forest. I don't know if this is the proper route, but I plunge onward.

The house appears in the distance. The stone farmhouse with the warm meals and the room full of beds. The place is lit up like an ocean liner. A silhouette of a boy waves to me from a bright upper window. I stall at the front gate with my hand on the latch, wary of the reaction to my return. A group of adults and older kids gathers in the yard. I can't recall their actual faces. The adults seem glad to see me and calmly tell me that dinner is waiting. Nobody acts as if anything strange has happened. An older woman with calloused hands helps me change into fresh clothes, then leads me into the kitchen. I sit by myself on a wooden stool at the counter. The vegetable soup is still hot.

I lie tucked in my bed in the large room. The bodies in the neighboring rows are already asleep. My eyes are shut, but I'm sifting the day's events for explanations. I suspect I'm remembering things wrong. Maybe nothing unusual happened after all. There is only the hypnotic sound of breathing, the enfolding comfort of clean sheets, the warmth of the wool blanket pulled to my eyes. This small drama approaches its end. The curtain begins its final descent.

No, wait, several nights later, I creep out of the pitch-black house, careful not to wake anyone. I venture back into the woods with a bulging backpack slung over my shoulders. I stubbornly trace a straight line through the landscape. Branches scrape my cheeks. Puddles soak my shoes. In the distance, several strays bay at the hidden moon.

The same clearing. The same sapling. I kneel on the soft grass in front of the backpack and unzip the inner pouch. Unfortunately there's no rope inside, but I do have several jars slopped full of runny and half-rotted leftovers. I sit with my back anchored against the tree and lather a thorough coating of food over my body. It smells pretty strong, a mix of syrupy perfume and tangy mold. Now I wait for the strays to return. I try to remember the exact shape of their eyes.

Every time the wind scatters the clouds, I howl at the white moon. As my throat grows hoarse, it sounds like a tortured yelp. I repeat it over and over, but nothing stirs. The woods remain hushed. None of the strays takes the lure. They keep their own counsel.

The tips of the grass swirl in complex patterns. The surrounding bushes creak and rattle. Then a man breaks into the clearing. He seems familiar though his features remain blank. He shakes his head at the sight of me slathered in leftovers. I wrap my arms around the tree trunk and refuse to leave, but I'm too exhausted to put up a memorable fight.

I ride through the woods on the man's back. My elbows rest on his shoulders, my legs dangle through his arms. The reliable rhythm of his steps rocks me toward sleep, though the feeling is less like settling into a dream than waking from one. The man lurches forward and I steady myself. My fingers fumble against a swath of fabric. He's wearing a mask.

Waves of darkness, created by swiftly moving banks of clouds, roll through the forest.

The lights of the stone house blink on in the distance.

I can't get rid of this smell.

CHAPTER 2
MY LIFE IN CAPTIVITY
(11 years old)

"The spilled drop, not the saved one."
–Eudora Welty

I STARE AT THE RICKETY HOUSE ACROSS THE street. The girl's bedroom is in the front: The window on the second floor with the black curtains. Usually she peeks out and stares at me with her round green eyes. She's been watching me for days, but rarely acknowledges my presence. Today she's refused to even make an appearance. Maybe she's angry at me for stealing the oranges.

I sit alone in the dining room and wait for her curtains to part. It's late afternoon. Slivers of sunlight filter into the room and gild the bookshelves surrounding the table. One beam falls on the bone china plate that holds the two oranges. An hour ago, I shimmied up the tree near the front door of the girl's house and plucked the only two ripe pieces of fruit.

A noise upstairs jars me out of my vigil. The sound of my mother's drunken footsteps rustling across the floorboards. It's been days since I've seen her. She circulates through the house like a ghost, bumping into furniture. We've been living here on the edge of the woods for 116 days, according to the secret tally I've been keeping on the back flap of the peeling rose wallpaper in the bathroom. Or maybe it's been longer. The tiny scrawls have almost merged into a single desperate slash. This is typical of our cycle. I've spent years moving from orphanage to orphanage. Every so often, my mother reappears to reclaim me. This time I'm eleven years old.

The curtains across the street flutter. I hold my breath waiting for the girl's pale face to emerge, but nothing happens. I'm so distracted that I don't notice the sounds in the house have grown louder. Then I realize my mother has appeared in the doorway. Something tells me to hide the oranges, but it's too late and I'm too hungry.

Her blouse is wrinkled and there's a stain on her pants. She clutches a crossword book in one hand and a glass of wholesale gin in the other. The alcohol threatens to slosh over the rim. She looks like she's been blacked out for days. "There you are," she says, as if I'm the one who's been missing. She runs her fingers lightly along my back. Her touch feels like it burns.

She sits across from me and opens the crossword book, wetting the pencil lead with the tip of her tongue while scanning the horizontals and verticals. She's been working on these puzzles forever but almost nothing has been filled in. The book is mostly white spaces and empty boxes. My mother silently eyes the oranges on the plate. It's impossible to tell what she's thinking. She doesn't realize I haven't had a real meal in days.

I start to peel one of the oranges with my fingers, digging my nails into the rind to create a seam that I can tear. My mother slaps my hand.

"Damn it, Jeff," she says. "I can't believe you don't know how to peel a fucking orange." She stands up and strides into the kitchen. While she's gone, I nervously pick the lint off my green sweater. The house across the street remains motionless.

My mother reappears with a squat silver knife with a curved crescent blade. She holds out her palm and I hand her one of my oranges. She cuts away ribbons of rind, then chops the remaining white off the fruit at sharp, elegant angles. There are no clinging flecks of rind, no skin left at all, it's shaved down to the juice, completely exposed. She places the glistening nude thing back on the plate. I've never seen anything so orange.

"Don't worry about keeping it exactly round," she says. "It'll find its own shape."

She slides the knife across the table.

"Your turn."

As I begin to sheer the skin from the second orange, the curtains across the street flutter again. The girl's hand pulls back the fabric and one green eye peers out. Then she vanishes.

"Don't be so delicate," my mother scolds. I've been carving the orange like a soap sculpture. I change tactics and hack off pieces with quick blunt strokes. It's pretty easy, actually. I place the peeled orange on the china plate. I brace myself for one of my mother's explosive rages, but she gives the fruit a cursory inspection and nods. Her highest form of praise.

She cuts both oranges into fat slices and takes a bite. I stuff an entire wedge in my mouth and slurp it down. It's tart but juicy.

"Not bad," she says. "Where'd you get them?"

"They gave them to me across the street."

"Enjoy them," she says. "You're never going over there again."

"Why not?"

My mother narrows her pupils and my blood chills. It's clear that she's contemplating throwing her glass of gin in my face. She raises her hand, but only takes another slice of orange.

"Because the man who lives there is a big fucking asshole," my mother says. Her slate gray eyes keep me in their grip. "He's a sex pervert. He just got out of prison and he'll probably be arrested again soon."

My mind races with this new information. All I can say is "okay." I try to figure out whether the girl is the man's daughter, or his niece, or something else entirely. I can't decide if her expression held any clues. Before I only imagined her life in that window, but now a whole frame crashes into place around it. Maybe the girl wants to escape and doesn't know how. As I take another bite, the fruit tastes different.

My mother turns back to her book of puzzles and hovers over a clue. I retrain my gaze on the girl's window. We both reach for slices of orange and absently consume them, bite by bite. Neither of us speaks a word. There's only the measured sound of our breathing. My mother tries out several letters, then sighs and erases them. The sun sinks low and I have to squint to see anything through the glare. It doesn't matter because the black curtains remain closed. Soon the china plate is empty. A sweet and acid odor lingers. I ball the loose orange rinds into a roughly round shape. Something lodges itself under my nails and I carefully study those last flecks of iridescent pulp.

■ ■ ■ ■ ■

The house across the street is empty. The moon spills a faint light across its front lawn. The night before the man left town, I saw the girl sprinting across this stretch of grass. She was wearing a pale nightgown with a dark stain. She ran swiftly and silently past the orange trees and toward the woods. Then she seemed to vanish. I can't stop thinking about her.

I lie in my darkened bedroom and stare out the window, fine-tuning my own plans to run away. This helps to keep my mind off the pain. It hurts every time I move. I'm lying on my stomach and can't see how serious the injury is, but I can feel the blistered skin. Somewhere between my shoulder blades there's a burn the shape of a clothing iron.

My mother enters the room with a jar of salve. She sits on the mattress and applies some to my bare back. It stings, so I grit my teeth and bury my face in the pillow. The wobbly swirl of her fingertips is a pretty good indication that she's still shit-faced.

"Sometimes I think you ruin my things on purpose," she says. "You have to learn how to do things for yourself. What are you going to do when I'm not around?"

There's no point in answering, so I don't.

She unrolls some gauze and lays it over the wound. She keeps adding layers, seemingly unsure how many are required. Her fingers poke and prod the sore while trying to fix tape to the edges. Once the bandage is secure, she turns on the bedside lamp to better examine her handiwork.

My mother starts to sob. She buries her face in her hands. Her entire body quakes. Wracking sounds. Uncontrollable. Normally I'd let the emotional storm blow over, but after a few minutes I reach out and rest my hand on her shoulder.

She slaps at me. "You little shit!" she shrieks. "Don't touch me!" Her eyes are stretched wide and her teeth bared.

She stomps down the stairs. I remain in bed with eyes shut tight, not daring to stir. I map her movements downstairs through the unsteady clomp of her steps. It's a radio play of stumbling sounds and muttered curses. She rustles from room to room, trying to remember her latest hiding place for the liquor. Rattling cabinets, unsticking drawers, scuffling across the wooden floor. Finally the jingling of a glass bottle and a loud belch.

My mother eventually lurches back up the staircase. The long pauses between steps are punctuated by the sound of swishing liquid. Her shadow briefly eclipses my doorway as she steers herself toward the master bedroom. Then there's a loud thud, shaking the frame of the house. The familiar sound of her limp body hitting the ground. There are no further noises. She must be out cold.

I ease myself up from the bed. From the closet, I pull out the bag where I've packed my clothes, the edges padded with wads of bills that I've siphoned off my mother. Through my window, the empty house across the street gives off a haunted glow. The curtains have been stripped from the windows and a bald light bulb burns in a hallway somewhere, dimly illuminating the remaining nothingness.

There are a few things left to pack, including my cassettes of favorite songs taped off the radio. One cassette is still lodged in my walkman. I slip on the earphones and press play. My head floods with the sound of blown-out amps, drilling drums, and the faintest hint of a woozy melody. It gives me a dose of courage.

Still something is missing. I venture into the hallway and spot my mother's feet sticking out from her bedroom. Her body is sprawled in a heap across the entrance, so I cautiously thread my steps through her arms and legs. It only takes me a second to find her nightgown, which is balled atop the dresser. It's ruined with the imprint of a hot iron where I got lost in a daydream and let it sizzle into the fabric.

I slip the nightgown over my head. It fits surprisingly well. I inspect myself in the mirror. The unfamiliar reflection is an echo of the ghostly girl who lived across the street. It feels as if I've tapped into some of her mysterious spirit.

I grab my bag and ease down the staircase. The creak of each step feels like an earthquake, the recoil of the wood louder than any aftershock. Behind me, my mother murmurs a series of primordial groans. She starts to slur out my name. I bound down the last steps and hurtle out the front door.

I'm running across the lawn. I peer over my shoulder and spot the hunched silhouette of my mother at the upstairs window. I try to imagine the scene from her point of view, looking down at the pale specter in the nightgown streaking through the yard. Instinctively, I head for the woods at the end of the block. Tonight the sanctuary of trees resembles nothing more than an immense and yawning darkness.

I pull up the folds of the nightgown as I run. It feels light and flowing. The wind rushes up and blows against my legs, ballooning the fabric around me. I'm almost there. I can feel myself becoming swallowed by the darkness. I can feel the grass blades licking the soles of my feet. With every step, I'm waiting to disappear.

CHAPTER 3
MY LIFE IN THE WOODS

(12 years old)

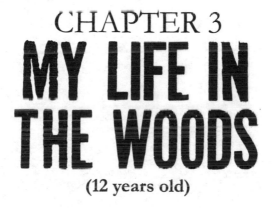

"Suddenly he was saying under his breath, 'We have a second home where everything we do is innocent.'"
–Robert Musil

I STALL AT THE EDGE OF THE CLEARING. FROM the shadow of the forest, I survey the scene. Plastic tents are ringed in the middle of a meadow. Along the perimeter, hammocks are strung between trees. The camp is mostly empty. Two girls race through the grass, waving lit sparklers. A couple of boys wrapped in wool blankets sit around a smoldering fire. Thin wisps of smoke rise in irregular puffs. I can't believe I'm finally here.

I'd heard stories about a tribe of teenagers who set up their own society in a remote part of the woods. A kid claimed to know the way and for fifty bucks scrawled a map on the back of an old Chinese take-out menu. I hitched rides along logging roads, hiked through overgrown paths, climbed steadily higher into the mountains. It's hard to remember exactly how I got here. And now that I've arrived, I'm not sure what to expect. I keep adjusting the pack on my shoulders. I wad the map into a tight ball. As I venture into the meadow, my entire body tingles.

The boys around the campfire greet me with easy smiles. The dogs sleeping in the grass bound up and lick my hands. Soon a few dozen teenagers emerge from the surrounding woods, returning from various chores and games. Everyone welcomes me to Liberia. We all gather firewood and share a dinner of lukewarm canned soup and petrified beef jerky. "You'll get used to the food," a girl with a ratty ponytail assures me. I find myself an empty woven hammock and fall asleep cocooned under a plastic garbage bag.

For the first week I'm there, it rains constantly. I help the kids with chores around the camp. The soles of my feet are perpetually soggy. The ghostly skin becomes so soft that I can scrape off ribbons of white flesh with my fingernail. Little mossy growths start to infest the scraggly hairs of my armpits. Even my cassettes begin to bloat with water and breed black spores. It's the happiest I've ever been.

When the weather clears, I start to explore the woods. I tag along with several kids and hike out to an abandoned wild kingdom theme park. It closed decades ago, but nobody bothered to knock down the cement outbuildings, dismantle the cages, or even strip the rusted tilt-a-whirl for parts. We climb the fence and roam the grounds, trying to guess which animals were kept where. The kids say that after dark it's popular to fuck in the cages. There's a rumor the place is haunted. Not by ghosts, but gibbons.

They tell me how the park's foreclosure dragged on so long nobody noticed when the monkeys escaped into the woods. They say the nearby towns have reports about the creatures attacking unsuspecting backpackers. Some kids believe these stories were invented to keep the truckers from bothering us. They say the truckers are worse than any gibbons. They brutally raped two girls who strayed too far from camp. Nobody could stop the bleeding.

Isaac swears the monkeys are out there. He's spotted their shadows in the dark trees, darting limb to limb. He even saw one up close, crouched on the rusty Ferris wheel and chomping on a jagged leaf. It had a pink nose and inflamed ass. Lydia says they might really be out there, but she's also been with kids who run through the forest and imitate the apes for a laugh. They scratch their pits and cling to low-hanging branches, whooping and yattering.

That night, I dream that I'm asleep in my hammock and awakened by a small white monkey. He perches on my chest and whispers stories to me, his furry mouth tickling my ear. He recites fantastical tales about his ancestors, the impregnable tree fortresses, the ornate weeklong banquets, the mysterious and coveted silver cup, the red poppy funeral garlands, the succession of betrayals that led to the tribe's ruin. In my dream, I'm convinced these stories contain the secret of my own destiny. As he unfurls his saga, the creature observes me with its kind golden eyes.

I awake with a start and expect to see the outline of a tiny monkey scampering into the recesses of the forest. But there's no evidence of any animal. The details of his stories have also evaporated from my memory. In the still of the night, I strain my ears for any sign but there's no hooting or gibbering, not even the pinched chatter of kids playing at being wild.

■ ■ ■ ■ ■

The truckers come with guns. They're drunk. Beefy red faces. Shallow pinprick eyes. They march into the center of camp and cock their rifles. All of them wear camouflage sweatsuits and orange flap jackets. It's hunting season. They say they'll give the kids a five-minute head start. To make things sporting. Maybe their original idea is only to scare the kids off the land. Watch them flee into the woods never to return. But the kids don't budge. One of the truckers fires a shot in the air and someone screams. A rock is hurled. Another shot. The kids turn around to find a pregnant girl lying on the ground with a bloody blown-out stomach. Then things get ugly.

The hunters' guns seem to fire at once. They explode throughout camp in a kaleidoscope of colors. Gleaming knives are drawn and brandished. The kids are in trouble and know it. They scatter in all directions. Kids running into the forest. Kids cowering behind trees. Kids with contorted mouths, red tongues lolling, screaming for help. Not that it makes any difference.

They're target practice. Bullets in the leg. Bullets in the chest. Bullets in the head. Crimson fountains of blood cascading into the air. The truckers are ruthless. Their thick black mustaches mask inscrutable emotions.

The kids beg for mercy. But the laws of decency are flouted. The truckers pour gasoline on the bushes and fan the day-glow orange flames. They saw off a boy's limbs. There are faces without eyeballs, slick gray organs tumbling loose from chests, a human head planted on a makeshift spike. The truckers fuck girls in the ass. They fuck girls in the nose. They fuck a boy in his detached arm socket. One trucker pisses shimmering yellow streams on the corpses nestled in somber hues of grass. It's a backwater holocaust. A bucolic apocalypse. A total extinction.

At least that's the story the painting tells. It's an enormous work that stretches across several canvases and it takes me a long time to absorb the details. The title: *The Ballad of Liberia*. Lydia created it over several months, hidden away in the woods, veiling her efforts under waterproof tarps. She unshrouds her masterwork in the meadow. Muted gasps are followed by an ecstatic round of applause. The thing is so over the top that everyone can't help but love it.

It isn't finished. Lydia has left some blank spots so people can express themselves, enter into the communal spirit, et cetera. We choose brushes and congregate around the long canvases. There's a hushed air of reverence as we confront the lurid and savage details of the painting. People move between the cans of paint and start applying respectful dabs of color. Some outline the carcasses in majestic shades of purple. Others plop shiny pink dollops on the cheeks of the living. A few jokers apply their strokes to the backside of the canvas.

Daniel throws the first handful of paint. A red splotch that hits Nycette square in the chest. Isaac retaliates by hurling a fistful of yellow at Daniel's face. Nycette pours purple paint on Isaac's head for being presumptive. The mohawked girl takes

Isaac's side and flicks paint at Nycette, but ends up splattering my pants instead. Then Daniel empties an entire can of blue down the mohawked girl's back. Just for the hell of it. And that's when pandemonium really breaks loose.

Soon everyone is coated with paint. Some kids take refuge behind the hammocks, retreat into the woods, launch counteroffensives near the river. Laughter and shouting echo throughout the camp. Lydia and I are the only ones left by the painting. She sits beside the canvas, arms wrapped around her legs, chin resting on her knees, sulking. Her white tank top is a fresco of smeared pigments. Her frizzy red afro looks more unruly than usual. "Do you have any idea how hard it was to drag that much paint out here?" she says.

She asks if I'm an art lover. I say not exactly. She says nobody else seems to be one either. I ask if she thinks the truckers might really attack the camp someday. She shrugs. "People are capable of anything," she says. While she adjusts the strip of silver duct tape that holds the bridge of her glasses together, her darting eyes give me a once-over. "You want to see my inspiration for the painting?" she says.

We hike through the forest to the abandoned theme park. She scouts to ensure nobody is lurking, then leads us past the empty cages toward the cement office buildings. They seem so boring I've never given them a second glance. In the back courtyard stands a narrow shed. A janitor's storage room of some kind. "I haven't shown this to anyone," she says. "It gives me nightmares."

The hinges of the shed are rusted shut, so she forces the door with her shoulder. It's a small concrete room with dingy gray walls. Cobwebs in every crevice. Dust motes choke the air. The light is so dim that at first the place looks empty. Lydia digs her nails into my arm and gestures at the corner. "People are bastards," she hisses. Then I see it. Against the back wall, pocked with scabby patches of gray mold, the mummified skeleton of a dog hangs from a noose.

■ ■ ■ ■ ■

The kids talk about the place in whispers. Everyone calls it the dead village, but the row of condemned houses on the edge of the woods is officially named Monrovia. It's a failed settlement that no longer appears on even the most local maps. Briefly converted into an outpost by the forest rangers, the houses are now abandoned. These once stately structures are marked by decay, wood rot, flood lines, and scattered rubbish. The only inhabitants are three girls who are reputed to have occult powers. Kids occasionally leave camp to visit them and have their fortunes told. Most are too spooked to make the journey.

Lydia says there's a treehouse that offers a view of the dead village. She leads a small group through the woods to see for ourselves. She blazes a fresh trail through the thick undergrowth of weeds and ferns. We follow the blue marks in the trees. They're painted in the hatchet scores on the tree trunks. Every few minutes another blue slash appears. It's the sort of code that you have to know to notice, a clandestine swath of color that beckons us forward.

None of us have laid eyes on the dead village. Isaac wonders what we'll be able to distinguish through the thick foliage. Daniel suspects the place gives off a subtle supernatural aura. Nycette believes the derelict houses have absorbed some of the properties of the oracles who now inhabit them. I find it hard to imagine anything more mysterious than our own campsite. Lydia remains silent. She maintains the steady pace.

The sky darkens. Storm clouds press down upon the treetops. The first raindrops start to sift through the branches. Soon we're soaked to the roots of our hair. Lydia says it's only another hour to the treehouse. Several people turn back, but the rest of us march onward. We tent our shirts over our heads and train our eyes on the boot prints in front of us. The booming bass of thunder resounds in our chests. Flashes of lightning bleach the air. More people peel off, but Lydia never turns around. Even the overstuffed backpack strapped to her shoulders doesn't slow her tempo. I'm not sure how long it takes her to realize that she and I are the only ones left.

Lydia halts in a clearing and peers up at the pelting rain. She wipes her frizzy red hair from her forehead and adjusts her glasses. I huddle beneath my sweatshirt and hug myself for warmth. "It's right around here," she says. She strolls under the trees, her head cocked toward their canopies, staring with the intensity of a hunter sighting game. She stops beneath a towering oak and signals to me. The treehouse is nestled high in its gnarled branches. We scale the wobbly rungs tacked to the trunk and squeeze through a narrow opening.

We find ourselves in a musty wooden room built with thick planks. Lydia lights the candles stationed in glass bowls along the floor. The place slowly takes on a cozy feel. Black garbage bags are tacked over the windows to keep out the elements. A stained mattress with rumpled sheets and a wool blanket is flopped in the corner. A sequence of faded magazine photos are taped to the wall: Shots of a naked couple walking hand-in-hand along the white sands of a beach. "I haven't been here in ages," Lydia says.

We're both soaking wet. Lydia searches her backpack for a towel but it's soggy as well. She instructs me to strip off my clothes and get under the blanket before I catch cold. I remove my T-shirt and jeans, but I'm too shy to take off my water-logged briefs. She laughs and precariously balances her thick black glasses on my nose. "You can hide behind these," she says. Everything appears slightly distorted, a filmy fish-bowl perspective. Lydia inspects how the glasses affect my features.

She kisses me. Her lips are rough and chapped. She peels

off her wet tank top. Her neck and arms are slightly sunburnt, making her breasts seem almost lunar in their whiteness. Her areoles are a soft crayon pink. There's a jumble of sensations: Her fingers through my hair, her tongue in my ear, her breasts in my mouth, her hand on my balls. Her wet skin feels slick against my body. She pushes us onto the mattress and straddles me. She slides me inside her and does all the work. I'm not sure whether I'm coming, but then I'm sure. We sink into the tangled covers and close our eyes. I don't tell her this is my first time.

For a long while, there's only the steady plink of rain against the roof. It's impossible to say how much time passes before I realize something is wrong. My fingers are coated in a warm fluid. A small dark stain is spreading across the filthy white sheets. I sit up and discover my crotch is coated in blood. My cock is bright rust red with dark splotches and uneven coagulations. I'm freaking out, but Lydia isn't the least bit alarmed. "Relax," she says. "I must have gotten my period."

I start to wipe myself clean with the sheets, but Lydia tells me to leave it. "It's perfectly natural," she says. "It's beautiful." She gets out of bed and squats over her backpack. Her perfectly round ass juts out like a baboon's while she rifles through the contents. She produces a weathered sheet of notebook paper and unfolds it with a solemn sense of ceremony.

She explains that an old boyfriend visited the dead village and returned with his fortune etched on this sheet. The page is scratched with a few barely legible phrases: *150 times*, *Northwest Passage*, and *The one you lost*. "It was a code written especially for him," Lydia says. "He was obsessed with it. The main oracle, this girl named Sara, she's the one who channeled it." She presses the paper into my hands. "You can tell it's the real thing," she says. "It almost vibrates." And it does. An uncanny pulsation thrums through the thin fibers of the page. Or maybe it's just my hands trembling.

Lydia says her boyfriend ultimately figured out the prophecy and vanished one night without any goodbye. "He went off to pursue his destiny or whatever," she says. She peels back one of the garbage bags to let the evening breeze filter through the window. She smoothes her red hair and stares into the final embers of the fading charcoal light. "I'm heading to the dead village tomorrow," she says. "You should come with me."

I'm not sure what to say. Somewhere outside the window are the sagging rooftops of Monrovia. I search for signs of life, but it's hard to make out even the most basic shapes among the surrounding branches. The hazy landscape appears to swim before my eyes. It's slightly disorienting. Then I remember that I'm still wearing Lydia's glasses. I hand them back to her. "I'm sorry," I say.

"Forget it," she says. "It was a dumb idea. More of a joke, really."

She produces a package of tinned sausages from her backpack. We eat in silence then blow out the candles. The treehouse feels smaller as soon as our shadows are scrubbed from the walls. Once in bed, she wraps the blanket around her tight as a shroud. In the middle of the night, snared in a dream, she makes faint growling noises. She clutches the oracle's note tight in her small fist. I'm overcome by an urge to pull her close, to kiss her neck, to whisper sweet things in her ear. But she doesn't stir and the urge passes and eventually I fall back asleep.

When I wake in the morning, Lydia's not there. I climb down from the treehouse and race into the woods. I shout her name but the only answer is the echo of my voice and the screech of some startled birds. Instinctively I know she's headed to Monrovia. I follow the blue spots on the trees, but I'm hesitant to go too far down the fog-obscured route. Before I return to camp, I spot the telltale signs. I kneel in the dirt and touch my finger to the series of her bitter-tasting droplets. The path to the dead village is marked by a fresh trail of blood.

■ ■ ■ ■ ■

We find the body at the bottom of the river. It has floated downstream and been snagged in the shallows by a dam of fallen
twigs and branches. A teenage girl, lying there submerged, bob-
bing peacefully in the gentle current, strands of long chestnut
hair mixing freely with the algae and underwater ferns. The first
thing we notice: She wears a nondescript pair of fraying jeans
and faded purple T-shirt. Second thing: None of us recognize
her. Third thing: A rope is fastened smartly around her bulging
neck.

It's a clear case of suicide. Or maybe murder. Daniel figures
the girl came to this remote sector of the woods to end it all in
solitude, dangling herself from a branch over the river. Isaac
thinks she was hiking into Liberia when some truckers inter-
cepted her, maybe raped her, definitely strangled her. Nycette
refuses to offer an opinion. She rolls herself a joint with trembling fingers and puffs away with fearsome determination. In
her penetrating French accent, she keeps repeating the word
"heavy."

Nobody bothers to ask what I think. I stare at my watery
reflection as it floats superimposed over the image of the
girl. She's flawlessly conserved in the cool current. Her lips a
perfectly serene shade of blue. Her pink tongue protruding
between her teeth, just so. Her eyes halfway open and unfocused
on something they couldn't see anyway. The expression on her
face would seem sexual, except it's too fixed to suggest any kind
of desire. She looks beautiful.

The four of us hover on the banks of the river, everyone
afraid to speak. Isaac finally announces that people at camp need
to be warned in case the truckers strike again. Daniel counters
that everyone is paranoid enough already and it's irresponsible
to panic them. They look to Nycette to cast the deciding vote,

but she throws up her hands in exasperation. In the background, I pace the points of an invisible triangle.

It's a stalemate. We leave the girl in the water and stare at her undulating corpse as if it's an aquarium exhibit. Nycette anxiously braids and rebraids her blond dreadlocks while getting profoundly stoned. Daniel repeatedly pops the cartilage in his oversized nose, the only part of him that doesn't conform with the suave pretty boy image. Isaac sits cross-legged on a tree stump, wearing an expression so serious that his features seem squeezed into a single dot at the center of his bald head. I anxiously skip rocks several yards downstream.

Isaac is the one who breaks the silence. "So tell me this," he says. "If we do keep it a secret, what the hell are we going to do with the body?" There's another long pause punctuated by the plinking skip of stones. It's Nycette who eventually answers. She exhales a fat plume of smoke. Her golden eyes are shining. "It is very simple," she announces. "We will burn it."

It turns out Nycette has done some reading about the rites and rituals of the Incas. According to what she remembers from a moldering anthropology text, the only honorable way to send off the dead is via funeral pyre. The flames release the soul from the cage of the dead person's body. Set it free to travel to the afterworld. Greet its maker with a purified slate. Something like that.

Isaac rolls his eyes at Nycette's spiritual talk, but this is obviously the perfect option. She reminds us that it's small-minded to demean the spiritual traditions of esteemed ancient civilizations. Daniel suggests we start gathering kindling moss and fallen branches right away and reconvene tonight. He seems pleased about our secret and makes everyone swear a blood oath to return alone.

The last thing we do that afternoon is dredge the body from the bottom of the river. We wade up to our shins, stoop into the current, and each grab a limb. A cloud of silver minnows bursts from beneath the corpse and swarms our feet. We lift on the count of three. A one and a two and—. Waterlogged and rigor-stiff, the girl is heavy as a slab of stone. We heave her onto the grass. Her inert body looks as incongruous as the sculpture of an anchor displayed on shore.

When I return that night, the fire is already a thick column of light. Daniel stokes the white-hot embers and slots several plank-like pieces of wood across the top. "This is going to be good," he keeps repeating to nobody in particular. He pulls his black mane into a ponytail and promenades around the blaze, surveying it from every possible angle. It's unclear whether he knows what he's doing or is simply excited to be in control.

Nycette smokes an extra-thick joint. Her pupils are tiny buoys of blackness in a sea of glitter. She stands over the body, confi-dently preparing the spirit inside for its journey to the heavens according to a set of half-remembered precepts. "We name her Mama Cocha," she says. "We give her the name of the Incan sea mother." She solemnly drapes her own shell necklace around the girl's swollen throat. It almost covers the purple ring of clotted bruises.

Isaac stands with his back to the fire. The rippling shad-ows make his features flicker like an old tube television caught between stations. "You're really okay with this?" he asks me. There is something unsettling about the ceremony, but I don't want to break rank with the group. So I shrug my shoulders and act as if none of it really matters.

Time to put the body on the pyre. Isaac refuses to touch it on the grounds that he's decided this whole idea is totally sick. So Nycette and Daniel hoist the corpse between them. They look queasy wrapping their fingers around the clammy, bloated limbs. The fresh air has accelerated the decomposition process. The body has pickled and the skin has started to suppurate. The mottled flesh is inhuman. They awkwardly swing the corpse back-and-forth to gain momentum. They toss it atop the fire.

It rolls off. The body lies face-down on the ground. Daniel and Nycette pick it up again, trying not to seem distressed. They get a firmer purchase on the arms and legs. Choose a better angle of approach. Pitch the body with more force. But it takes three more tries before the dead girl lies on her back atop the pyre. Her empty face stares up at the blinking stars. Flames conflagrate beneath her body, separated by only a few wooden planks. It's a breathtaking sight. The girl looks almost majestic. I think that claptrap about the spirit might be true after all.

Then the stench. As the flames blacken the boards and catch the corpse, they unleash a consuming odor. A mixture of the raw and the curdled: Overripe fruit and mold spores; singed hair and meat rot; fresh blood and smeared shit. There's a perfume-like undercurrent, a sweet tang that's briny. It's the sort of smell you can only fully register in the back of your throat as you start to gag. I smother my face with my shirt and retreat to the edge of the clearing.

Isaac screams: "Somebody take the body off the fire." He hops in a mad circle around the flames, trying to leap close to the pyre without getting burned. Panic blurs his features and there's a horrified glaze to his eyes. "C'est impossible to stop," Nycette says. "Her spirit is still trapped inside." And it really is too late. The girl's body is completely charred. She's a glowing cinder.

I shimmy up a tree to escape the smell. This is my first funeral. As I watch, part of me wants to obliterate the experience from my memory but part finds it exhilarating. I can't take my eyes off the blaze. It's several minutes before I realize what's missing: None of us are grieving. Daniel grimly stokes the fire, determined to finish the job. Nycette chants a round of basic incantatory stuff, trying to splice into some primeval spiritual current. Isaac curses us all and flees into the woods.

The body ignites. It ruptures into a mass of flames, followed by a sickening pop. "There she goes," Nycette shouts. The corpse is completely alight, an incandescent effigy, starting to flake off into swirling sheets of gray. The putrid smell continues, lifted by the flames and carried in the smoke toward the firmament. Ash rains down like confetti on Nycette and Daniel. They are coated from head to toe in flecks of burnt skin, but they hardly seem to notice, staring up at the sky, tracing the soul's journey home, marveling that something up there might be looking back at them. Their upturned faces are beatific and shining.

While Nycette and Daniel are fixed in their private rapture, I leap down from the tree and slip into the woods. I need to be alone. I spend the night curled under a canopy of ferns in a clearing upstream. No matter how many times I tell myself to stop thinking about the girl's face submerged in the cool blue current, the horrid pop of her body won't stop echoing in my ears.

In the following days, the other kids in camp avoid Daniel and Nycette. Both their bodies give off a rank and fleshy odor. Even the canines aren't sure how to deal with the smell; their carrion instincts are scrambled and they can't decide whether to make a move. Nycette and Daniel are too pleased with themselves to care. They're often seen together on nightly strolls talking cosmology in the meadow. A pack of dogs always trails a few paces behind, their noses vibrating.

■ ■ ■ ■ ■

After the cremation, I start thinking it might be time to leave Liberia. The idea appears one morning, like the sticky residue of a forgotten dream. I pull on my damp socks. Swallow a few teeth-pulls of beef jerky. Roll up my hammock with the plastic sheet inside as carefully as if it were a pastry, spend the morning wandering through the muddy ravines of camp, not meeting anyone's gaze, hands sunk in the pockets of my rotting jeans, feet scuffing the spongy ground, feeling like I'm already half gone. Even my footprints seem lighter.

That afternoon I pack my bag. I know where I'm headed. I scale the chain-link fence and scout the perimeter. Nobody is around. I creep through the empty grounds, careful to avoid the cement janitor's shed. I run a moss-covered branch along the bars of the cages, soothed by the metallic reverberations. I wonder what the animals remembered of their time here. On a lark, I squeeze inside one of the cages. Sniff the dirt to determine what creature lived here, but there is no tang of musk or finely scented urine. I make myself at home. Pace back and forth. Hop up and down. Swing arms from side to side. Make chattering and hooting noises. But the play-acting seems half-hearted, even to myself.

While I hang upside down from the bars, someone strides past the cage. He doesn't seem to notice me. I follow at a discreet pace as he heads toward the overgrown arcade where the carnival rides once thrived. Only a few dilapidated husks now remain, their paint faded to a sickly pallor, peeling and infested with scabs of rust. They're like misshapen boulders deposited by some receding glacier. The boy marches into the ring of dirt where the carousel once sat. He kneels at the center of the circular pit and starts to dig.

Crouched in some scrubby bushes, I can't see his face. The boy methodically scoops out a small hole with his hands. He slides a bag off his shoulder and removes a yearbook snapshot of a teenage girl flashing a stiff half-smile. He places it in the hole and smothers it with dirt. The boy pulls out a series of small china plates, none larger than a sand dollar. He arranges them in a precise circumference around the hole. The remaining contents of the bag are scavenged scraps of food half-eaten apple, moldy dinner roll, frayed threads of beef jerky—which he lays on the plates as if setting out a meal.

Entranced by this private ritual, I forget myself and rustle the bushes. The boy wheels around. It's Isaac. A contorted expression of anger and desperation ripples across his face. For a second, he looks like a colicky baby before it screams. But then his features snap back into blankness. He motions to join him in the carousel pit. I feel weird about interrupting, but he's insistent.

"My girlfriend killed herself three years ago today," Isaac says. "She overdosed by swallowing a bottle of pills. Not many people know that." I give an empathetic nod, as if I can possibly understand. We sit together with our legs crossed Indian-style. My eyes are trained on the white plates, two of which are still missing food. Isaac doesn't offer any explanations. His fingers knead the lip of a plate, as if trying to conjure sound from the ceramic grooves.

There's something about this strange and touching offering that makes me realize what I need to do. I start to offer Isaac my condolences about his girlfriend, but instead I blurt out: "I'm leaving Liberia tonight. I'm going to the dead village. To the oracles."

I expect him to try and talk me out of it, but instead he offers a weary smile. He sets about completing his ritual, taking the last gnarled strands of beef jerky and positioning them on the empty plates. As he surveys the circle of food, his expression oscillates between anxiety and melancholy. I dig inside my knapsack for the filthy plastic bag filled with crushed blackberries. My favorite meal. "I'd like to add something," I say.

"You'll need those for your trip."

"It's okay," I say. "I want to." I'm not sure why but I know it's important to make a contribution. With an appropriate sense of ceremony, I kneel next to the china plate that holds only a half-gnawed crab apple and slowly shake the berries from the bag. They form a soggy black pyramid and spill over the plate, which is soon encircled in a pool of purple juice. "For your girlfriend," I say.

Before Isaac can respond, we hear crackling sounds and

hushed twitters from the bushes and trees. The leaves shudder. Fleetingly familiar shapes dart through the foliage. Isaac stares into the underbrush, gradually working his gaze round the perimeter. "They're here," he says. "We'd better go now."

Without seeing them, I can feel their presence. The small faces, hairy paws, arched tails. "They're real," I say.

"Quiet," Isaac says. "Back away slowly. Don't spook them." We take a series of deliberate and measured steps toward the entrance of the midway, as if this too is part of the ritual. The whistling whoops and belly growls begin to escalate. A shiver ripples through my body. I imagine a mass of furry backs hunched in the shadows, anxious for us to leave so they can swarm the plates and devour their offering. We keep walking with our gazes trained on the ground, but I can tell we're encircled by countless pairs of tremulous golden eyes.

■ ■ ■ ■ ■

The dead village is silent. A hushed crowd waits inside a decaying house to see the oracles. We huddle along the wooden staircase and stare up at the water-stained ceiling. Black mold spreads in fern leaf patterns across the plaster walls. A fractured kitchen sink rests at the end of the hallway. A partially disassembled motorboat engine lies in the bathtub. The pilgrims are a combination of vagrant tourists and weary travelers. Most of these patient souls have been waiting for hours. I've been here longer than any of them.

Their door is locked, but I peer through the keyhole and spy the oracles lost in their dreamy duties. Three pale girls in pink nightgowns with white athletic socks pulled over their knees. One oracle spoons mossy grounds into a trio of mismatched cups. Another lifts a kettle from an electric hot plate and sniffs the steam rising from its spout. The third removes the lid from a red sugar bowl and inspects the contents. The girls hover wordlessly around the steeping tea. Their shoulder blades twitch involuntarily. I'm not supposed to be watching this.

There's the click of the lock. The squawk of the rusty hinges sounds as startling as a shipyard whistle. Two of the oracles appear in the door frame. Their sinewy faces are almost ecto-morphic. Their condor eyes survey the crowd and seem vaguely unsatisfied with the tally. Each holds a glass ashtray filled with damp tea leaves. Everyone around me plays it cool, as if they're parishioners at some rote worship service. I'm not so suave. My heart starts to sweat. "We're ready to begin," the two oracles announce.

I'm the first in line but let the skinhead girl with the book-ish glasses take my place. The crowd pushes me into the room behind her and a flock of us hover along the nearest wall. We observe the main oracle who sits in the center of the room, a black notebook nestled in the folds of her nightgown. This must be Sara. There's nothing particularly striking about her chubby figure and greasy brown hair, but she radiates an otherworldly air of detachment.

The skinhead girl kneels in front of Sara's chair. One of the assistant oracles dabs a brown smudge of tea leaves on the girl's forehead. Sara props a foot on the girl's shoulder and presses her thumb into the spot. Her eyes turn milky white and her free hand begins to write. The pen moves at its own pace, the strokes slowly accumulating across the page. When the writing ceases, Sara rips out the sheet with a flourish. The message reads: *22, 7, 16. Bobbie Merlino.* It's unclear from the skinhead girl's reaction if the information has significance, but she creases the paper with painstaking care before tucking it inside her plastic billfold.

I let the black teenager with the infected nose-ring go next. As Sara enters her trance, I catalog the spartan contents of the bedroom. Bare mattress arranged on the wooden floor. Oval mirror draped with black velveteen. Peeling sea-green wallpa-per with sun-faded sailboats navigating toward some unknown port. Sara finishes inscribing the notebook page with a map and marks an X in the upper left-hand corner. The text reads: *This is where you will kill your father.* The boy acts unfazed but his eyes keep blinking at the paper, perhaps hoping a different message will materialize.

I signal the man with the grizzled beard to take my place, but one of the assistant oracles seizes my elbow. She motions for me to kneel in front of Sara, but instead I keep stalling. There's so much that suddenly needs explaining. I want to tell her the history of my life and ask her what destiny the stars have been cooking up for me, but I can't find the syllables. I can only stammer out the most basic information: "My name is Jeff Jackson."

Sara's lashes flutter, as if she's struggling to bring a strange specimen into focus at the end of a microscope. She appears slightly cross-eyed, her brown orbs unsuitable for everyday tasks. Her semi-blank stare reminds me of a crab whose stalks twitch in the direction of the nearest noise.

I kneel in front of Sara's chair. She splays her legs and places a foot on my shoulder. I glimpse a few curly pubic hairs sticking out like orchid tendrils from the cotton crotch of her panties. One of the assistant oracles applies the warm tea leaves to my forehead. A brown rivulet of resin slips down the tip of my nose. It probably looks like my third eye is weeping. Sara presses her thumb against the leaves.

The spot instantly feels white-hot, an intense burning pressure, as if a hole is being bored through the bone of my skull. I bite my tongue to keep from shouting. I focus on Sara's pen as it moves across the page in swift and soundless strokes. The only noises come from the rhythmless plink of the rain, the jittery clank of the ancient steel radiator, the thin whistle of static from an unseen radio. The pen halts and Sara tears the page from her notebook and hands it to me. The sheet is blank.

A tense murmur wafts through the house. More people squeeze inside the room. Someone asks me to display the sheet and it produces an eerie silence, as if I were an executioner raising his victim's head above the crowd. Nobody wants to tell me that the last person who received a blank page from Sara died soon afterward. Nobody wants to explain that it's akin to drawing the tarot card of the skeleton astride his emaciated steed. One of the assistant oracles leans close and whispers, "I'm sorry." All eyes are set on me. Only Sara's gaze is elsewhere, transfixed by the coastline of torn paper that clings to the margins of her notebook.

The blank sheet sticks out of my back pocket. I stand on the lone strip of road and stare up at the oracles' house. A tireless rain spits from the sky and puddles around my feet. My clothes are soggy. My lungs burn. It stings every time I cough. The curtains of the upstairs window are closed, but eventually Sara will have to show her face.

I scoop several handfuls of wet gravel. It's easy to find ammunition in Monrovia. Everything is in ruins: the rotting porches, fallen tree limbs, incinerated automobile husks. Even the road I'm standing on—an aborted strip of asphalt that runs through the center of the village and evaporates before it reaches the woods—comes apart under your fingernails.

My first throw misses by several inches. The second ricochets off the sill with a dull clatter. But the third strikes a direct hit, the pebbles rattling brightly against the second-story window pane. There's no way she's not hearing this.

Eventually the curtains part and Sara appears in the window. She flits there for a few seconds, her plump palm resting flat against the pane. Her gaze runs straight through me as if I'm already dead. I shout her name, but the only thing that answers me is a warm handprint on the glass that's already beginning to evaporate.

The wind blusters in a succession of frigid gusts. My face is raw and chapped. My hands won't stop trembling. It feels like I'm coming apart. I launch another fistful of gravel at the window. The stones jangle off the rotten wooden siding, but none of them even scrapes the second floor.

"Your aim is for shit."

It's the skinhead girl. She adjusts the tips of her horn-rimmed glasses as if trying to bring my curious activity into better focus. The rest of the road is empty, but the other kids must be watching, too. Hosts of them are squatting in the surrounding derelict bungalows. It's easy to imagine their round faces, like balls on strings, suspended in the dirty windows. I let the rest of the pebbles sift through my fingers.

"You freaked out by the blank page?" the girl asks.

"Of course not," I say. "It doesn't have to mean something bad."

"That so?"

"Maybe it's like my destiny is still wide open. Nothing's been written yet. Everything is still up to me. That's pretty good, right?"

"So why are you out here in the rain throwing rocks at their window?"

I start to sneeze. Violent, hunched over, full-body sneezes. My eyes are red and watery. My entire body aches. The skinhead girl opens her umbrella and holds it over us. The raindrops thrum against the plastic canopy and it sounds like all the pebbles I've lofted into the air are slowly tumbling down on my head. "Maybe they made a mistake," she says softly.

"It's no big deal," I say. "Just some old sheet of notebook paper." I pluck the page from my back pocket and stretch it between my hands. I find myself holding it up like a blank billboard toward Sara's window. My fingers are quivering.

"You're getting it wet," she says.

I crush the paper into a wad and toss it on the ground. With the toe of my shoe, I stamp on it and rub it apart. The soggy sheet breaks into smaller and smaller pieces, until there's nothing but hundreds of dirty white flecks that resemble the rubbery shavings of an eraser.

A small audience of onlookers has gathered on the edges of the road. They stand with eyes averted, as if they've just witnessed some tragic event and are trying to downplay its importance. More people leave the abandoned houses and venture into the rainy street in twos and threes, covering their heads with bags and old newspapers. I figure they're coming to offer advice or consolation about the blank page, but they push past me and flock toward the oracles' porch. They all begin to file inside.

"Time for the nightly concert," the skinhead girl says. "Maybe you can talk to Sara after the show." She grabs me by the wrist and leads me toward the entrance.

Everyone has assembled in the living room, huddling on sagging couches, squatting on scratchy wool blankets, standing with backs hugging the plaster walls. A sickly sweet jasmine incense fills the air and masks the stench of stale sweat. A semi-circle of candles provides the light. The melted wax marks off the stage area, spreading like tree roots across the warped floorboards.

I sit on a coffee-stained sofa, balanced on wobbly box springs that threaten to uncoil. It feels like I'm getting sicker by the minute, alternating between face-reddening fever and teeth-chattering chills. Maybe I really am dying. People's gazes circle back to me with vulturous curiosity.

The room hushes. Three pairs of white athletic socks appear through the slats of the staircase, then the oracles swish their nightgowns and make a full-bodied entrance. They assume their place at the center of the candlelit circle. The two assistants throw their arms open and announce: "We are The Chorines!"

Muted whoops, muffled applause, a stray whistle.

This time the oracles don't seem so imposing. The nylon threads of their pink nightgowns shine from constant wear. Their cuticles are stained ochre from smoking hand-rolled cigarettes. They pick the gum from their teeth. They unfold the tops of their socks and scratch the inflamed insect bites on their calves. They let the silence of the room deepen.

Then The Chorines shut their eyes, clear their throats, and start to sing. Their throats vibrate together in a simple wordless tune. The voices circle one another according to an undetectable logic until they settle on a single resonant note. The sound builds to an immersive drone. The walls of the room begin to vibrate. It defies understanding how such a huge noise can radiate from the bodies of these three girls.

The audience seems to know what to do. They begin to join the song, fixing their voices to the choir, one person at a time. They start in the far corner and work their way around the room. Soon it feels like I'm in the middle of a hive. With each new voice, the delirious hum grows more intense.

Despite myself, I get goose bumps. Tears streak my cheeks. The buzzing inside my chest is perfectly attuned to the vibration of the music. Maybe this song is a sort of funereal requiem. Maybe it's meant for me. Sara stares purposefully in my direction. An emotional current surges between us that's understood only by the raised hairs on the back of my neck.

I begin to tremble. My breathing becomes shallow. I part my lips to join the chorus but no sound comes out. I'm choking. My throat gags. My arms and legs convulse. My body pitches itself onto the floor. The voices slowly break apart and a gallery of curious faces hovers overhead, their overlapping shadows smothering me like a blanket. Only Sara continues to sing, that one blissfully sustained note held by her open mouth.

I regain consciousness in a darkened storeroom. It's piled high with bundles of instruction manuals, cases of empty green bottles, and the propeller from a small crop duster. My body is crumpled in the corner, bundled in musty beach towels. The entire house is still. I listen to the clattering music of a thunderstorm pelting the roof and the wind whipping against the windows. Somewhere overhead I start to make out the soft sounds of a late-night colloquium. The voices of the oracles.

Maybe we should have a viewing... But what if he's not... We didn't do anything the last time it happened... There could be a cool ceremony... Yeah, you might as well invite the cops... Maybe it's easier to pitch him in the river... But what if he's not... We could have roses everywhere and pennies on his eyes... But what about afterward... There's always the garbage dump... But what if...

I let out a series of soft moans. The voices overhead trail off into silence. Soon there's the sound of tiptoed steps skulking down the hallway. Sara appears in the doorway with crossed arms and observes me. My forehead blazes. Every hair root on my head is a pinprick of pain. The hum of the song still rings in my ears. Eventually I find the words that have been circling my mind for most of the day. I wheeze: "Did the last person who got the blank sheet really die?"

"That's right." Sara's speaking voice is unexpectedly harsh, a pinched nasal twang. "Not every prophecy comes true. But that one sure did."

I say: "Maybe there was a mistake this time."

I say: "How about another reading."

I say: "I don't want to die."

Sara chews her lip. In the faint glow filtering through the window from some distant street lamp, her lovely features appear almost embryonic. It's as if her body has cultivated an ability to erase traces of emotion, the way unprimed canvas absorbs paint. "I'll give you a second reading," she says. "But you have to promise you won't tell anyone."

I nod, but she's not finished.

"And you leave tomorrow morning," she says. "I never want

to see your sorry ass again. If there are even rumors that you're lurking nearby, you'll regret it."

My fevered mind traces Sara's path back upstairs by the diminishing echo of her footfalls. She's greeted by the tense murmurs of the other oracles. This time their conversation is more discrete, volleys of whispers discharged like soft fireworks. They all seem to be pacing at once. Several minutes pass before the trio arrives in the storage room, the assistant oracles ferrying candles to better light the proceedings. In her upturned palms, Sara cradles the red sugar bowl. She calls us to order by rattling the ceramic lid against the edges as if it were a bell.

Sara tips the contents of the bowl onto the wooden floor. It's a collection of neon yellow capsules. She pinches a pill between her thumb and forefinger. It's embossed with a smiley face. "We use these to tell the fortunes," she explains.

"They're pretty mind-blowing," one of the assistants adds.

As Sara selects the pills, my fevered mind hits upon an idea. "If I took it, could I see my future?"

Sara and her assistants exchange a look that's more complicated than I am right now. "I guess so," Sara says. "But it's a bad idea. Most people can't handle it."

"I want to take it."

The assistants shake their heads but Sara remains noncommittal. She squeezes her eyes shut and sucks in her cheeks. Finally she hands me the capsule. "There's no guarantee you'll get a different reading," she says.

I balance the smiling capsule in my sweaty hand. It seems to be winking. Patches of dye rub off the edges. A yellow stain spreads across my palm like a rash. I try to calculate the odds the pill could be hazardous, then I take a deep breath and swallow it. It has a distinct sweet-and-sour aftertaste.

Now there's nothing to do but wait. The house is eerily still. The rain pounds a frenetic tattoo against the windows. Droplets of water accumulate in a remote corner of the attic. Mice burrow deeper into the soggy folds of insulation. The wooden planks groan in concert with the barometric pressure. Dust motes gently blanket the furniture, moldings, and floorboards. After a few minutes, my vision starts to cloud and the edges of the storage room whiten. At first I think I'm going blind, but then I realize there's nothing to fear. A veil is being lifted. I watch as the house transforms itself around me. The paint on the walls, the furrowed lines of my palms, the oracles huddled in the hallway with their twitching shoulder blades—everything is slowly becoming blank.

I CONTINUE

I record the events of my life, filling up one notebook after another. Maybe I'm not getting the details exactly right, but it doesn't matter. The strict facts hold no currency here. What counts is the saliva I just spat on this very sheet of paper. The thick gob slowly dissolves a small circle in the text and turns the words translucent. The ink starts to bleed. The fibers loosen. If you run your fingers along this paragraph, you'll feel the site where I stabbed my thumb straight through the page. There is an entire world in that hole.

CHAPTER 4
MY LIFE IN THE CITY

(14 years old)

"All true freedom is dark."
–Antonin Artaud

THERE'S THIS TAPE. IT ARRIVES ONE MORNING IN the mail, which is surprising because I don't have an address. I'm between places, as they say. Specifically, I'm shuttling between a cardboard refrigerator box in the alley next to the Emerald Mountain Chinese restaurant and a wool blanket on the concrete floor of the municipal shelter. But the mailman hand-delivers the package to me just the same. I'm coiled half-asleep in my box and he leaves it at my feet.

This is just the latest in a string of strange happenings in the neighborhood. The Luchos have relocated to these scabby streets and started marking their territory. Every morning freshly shattered glass shimmers on the sidewalks like dew. Kids casually cross the avenue with newly stolen car batteries tucked under their arms like purses. There are stories about winos waking up to bloody incisions and missing kidneys. Someone set a pack of wild dogs loose to roam the rooftops. At night, you can hear them hunting the local cats.

When I spot the package, I let out an involuntary yelp. But it's nothing more than a small parcel wrapped in brown paper and addressed in a blue magic marker scrawl that reads: "The Kid in the Alley behind the Chinese Place on 1st Avenue." I can't recall if I've ever received mail here before. I'm curious but hesitate to pick it up. For the months I've been living in the city, I've been trying to avoid any intrigue. I'm still struggling to navigate these streets. My world consists of a few square blocks and ritual activities. My focus is keeping body and soul intact.

I open the package with shaky fingers. This cassette tape is a genuine audio relic, tattered and beat-up, but someone decorated it with obvious care. A piece of notebook paper is neatly folded inside the plastic case and a dozen song titles are inscribed in a barely legible hand. Despite myself, the gesture touches me. It isn't some menacing totem, it's a gift. The first present I've received in ages. Of course I don't have any way to play it. So I depart straightaway to see Mister Pastor, the man with all the gadgets and a heart large enough to share them with the likes of me.

The park is nearly vacant. The sky is pitch gray. A chill wind blows loose litter over the concrete pavers, spreading it in even coats. A few homeless have bothered to climb the chain-link fences that protect the partitions of dead grass from the public. They lie sprawled on the ground like neglected sculptures, blackened by the elements. I make my way toward the band shell, a scalloped steel structure as rusted as everything else. Mister Pastor always camps next to the stage in an elaborate compound assembled from shopping carts, cardboard, and plastic sheeting. I kick the side to announce my presence and wait.

The only person nearby is a skeletal old man in a frayed long-coat and stained polka-dot bandana crouched in front of a baby stroller. He makes faces at the child, popping out his yellow dentures with his tongue, and contorting his features into a hideous rictus. The kid somehow remains silent. There's no parent in sight. This is a typical vista.

It takes a few minutes for Mister Pastor to appear. He's decked out in the usual: black knit hat that barely corrals his not-so-natty dreads, mirror sunglasses, and rumpled tan raincoat. Apparently I've woken him because he's launched into a diatribe that isn't quite under his breath. "Damn it, Jeff," he mutters. "Why the ofays always bothering the Pastor."

"Somebody sent this to me," I say. I lay the cassette in his massive hand for inspection. He turns it over several times, measuring its heft and testing its tactile properties.

"You know who it's from?"

I shake my head.

"And you're not concerned about that?"

"It's a gift," I say.

Mister Pastor looks at me incredulous. Like: How stupid can you be? I blankly return his stare: Pretty fucking stupid.

He shakes his head and trains his gaze back on the tape, probing the thing like it's some sort of voodoo totem, careful not to disturb its latent powers. "I'd throw this away if I was you," Mister Pastor says. "Right now."

"I don't know," I say. "I kind of want to hear it first."

Mister Pastor purses his lips so hard that his whole face seems to pucker as if what he has to express could barely be contained by all that bunched flesh. "Guess you must be the boss of you," he says finally. "So what do you need from me?"

"Walkman," I say. "So I can listen."

He sighs and ducks back inside the mouth of his compound. While he rustles through his array of cinched plastic bags and canvas totes, I turn away so I won't see where he stores his treasures. Etiquette. He reappears with a decrepit-looking walkman, both headphones missing their foam casings. "Plays fine," he says. "Just can't fast forward or rewind."

I want some privacy so I amble toward the green benches next to the empty dog run. The wind swirls some grimy black condoms and muddy supermarket fliers round my feet. I sit under a clump of bare trees, slide the tape into the player, and place the plastic headphones against my chilly ears. I look closer at the handwriting on the case—the series of curlicues, dashes, odd slants and sudden emphases—and for the first time truly begin to wonder who sent this.

I press play. It takes about fifteen seconds. The first strums of the acoustic guitar and then the onslaught of rattling drums and ragged horns all at once. And that voice. Oh my God, that voice. I sit transfixed. By the time the majestic echoing chords of the last song fade, something inside me has permanently shifted. Listening to this music is like being turned inside-out and finding the story of your life written on your inner organs. It's like having your blood leeched to remind you that you have blood. It's like—

The tape ends. I flip it over and play it again. And again. The singer sings with an inhuman urgency. He tells his story running and you can almost hear the clip of hooves in pursuit. He spins out tales of drunken fathers too scared to commit suicide, mute twins in white dresses spilling their parents' ashes over a frothing ocean, dead girlfriends reincarnated as black swans, or blue orchids, or flaming pianos. After a while, it's hard to keep it all straight.

Someone shouts from across the park. I switch off the music. I'm surprised to find that I must have been crying because tears stream down my cheeks. Plus there's this faint tang in the air, a damp and acrid odor. I look at my feet. The ground is covered in fresh, grayish-green splatches of pigeon shit. I look at my coat. It's caked in moist gobs of the stuff. No idea how long I've been sitting like this.

More shouts. I turn in their direction but it takes my eyes a few moments to focus. A gang of Luchos strides toward me. Six of them in black parkas, lumberjack boots, and doo-rags. Behind them, a fat plume of smoke billows from the side of the band shell where Mister Pastor is camped. A pack of dogs barks somewhere nearby.

The smart move would be to sprint headlong for the park gates. But instead I keep my ass flat on the bench, transfixed by the cassette case. I feel like I'm on the cusp of decoding its mystery and afraid to take my eyes off the handwriting. The signature lean of the letters, the yawning "o" that seems open in a shout, the frenetic "w" that hurries past with barely a nod. These are clues.

A thick gob of saliva lands at my feet. The Luchos. They ring the bench, glowering like a surly Greek chorus. One smacks his glossy lips and another rubs the vacant white orb where his cornea used to be. I try to look casual while scouting for potential help. The only person in sight is an elderly woman in a babushka combing the grass for discarded crack vials. A pack of dogs sniffs around her, nipping each other's asses.

Some quick options: *Run.* Not fast enough. *Fight.* Six against one. *Scream for Mister Pastor.* Judging by the fire at the band shell, I have a sinking feeling about that one, too.

The tallest Lucho—El Lucho Jefe—removes his doo-rag, signifying serious business. A thin ridge of bone runs along the top of his scalp, giving him an almost prehistoric profile. I tense. Pure animal reflex.

"Hand it over," El Lucho Jefe says. His voice is a droning hiss. He balls the doo-rag in his oversized knuckles.

I blankly return his stare.

"The walkman," El Lucho Jefe says. "That's ours."

There is only one acceptable response here. All other possible combinations of words are clustered above the same trap door and invite the same vertiginous fall. I brace myself. "It's not yours," I say.

"You sit in this park," El Jefe says. "Then it's ours." He smiles, revealing incisors that have been filed to sharp points.

I look at the cassette case in my palm and the tape slotted into the walkman. That voice. The handwriting. My gift.

"You can't have it," I say.

"Excuse me?" El Jefe says. He cracks his neck. A theatrical gesture, hand twisting neck to the side; it's accompanied by the loud pop of impacted bone.

"I said, you can't have it." Normally I skirt beatings whenever possible, but this time is different. Looks fly among the Luchos.

As they silently confer over this unexpected turn, I hoist myself onto the back of the bench. Better leverage in case of attack. For one wild moment, I think of the tape as a grenade that I can hurl at the ground and obliterate the entire gang with a brilliantly loud detonation. I zip the cassette and walkman inside my jacket.

El Lucho Jefe clears his throat. "I'm gonna say this one more—"

I lunge and knock him to the ground. Before he can react, I sink my teeth into his nose and clamp onto it as hard as I can. He screams and tries to throw me, but I hold onto his head and bite down harder. No idea where I get the idea or the ferocity. Maybe it's something from one of the songs.

The other Luchos awkwardly try to pull me off, unsure whether this is causing El Jefe more pain. His nose is squelchy cartilage in my mouth. I can feel it start to give. So can he. More screams. More cursing. I bite down harder. Around us the Luchos are barking like furious dogs. With a savage jerk, I rip my head to the side. His nose is in my mouth. A chunk of spindly, rubbery gristle. There's less blood than you'd think. Everything halts for a moment as El Lucho Jefe gives a heart-shuddering, high-pitched shriek to the heavens. I spit his nose on the ground.

This is when I first notice the pack of dogs has swarmed us. A teeming mass of thick-necked mutts, growling and gnashing their teeth. The Luchos who aren't clustered around the writhing El Jefe lunge at the animals and fight them to reclaim that forsaken lump of flesh.

I tear off down the nearest pathway. The loose soles of my sneakers slap against the concrete as I sprint for the park gates. My precious cargo is still zipped inside my jacket, cuffing against my heart as I run. Two frothing mutts are fast on my tail.

I dash out of the park and spy the wall of a community garden across the street. As I scuttle up the steel fence, one of the dogs snaps at my calf. I give it a ringing kick to the jaw and climb higher. A metal barb peels off the knee of my jeans. More scraped skin. Huffing and wheezing, I finally pull myself to the top of the fence. The dogs pace below with bared teeth. They have me tree'd but I don't care.

It turns out I'm pretty high up. A panorama of the entire park unfolds before me. Thick veils of smoke still heave from beside the band shell. The Luchos limply drag El Jefe toward the far avenue to hail a taxi. A handful of people lie face-down on patches of lawn. One of them, the elderly woman in the babushka, is dead. Not sure how I know, but somehow, from up here, I can tell.

Black storm clouds mass overhead. A sour wind stings my eyes. The dogs continue their angry vigil, but I'm no longer afraid. I remove the walkman from my jacket and play the cassette from the beginning. I squeeze my skinned knees together against the fence and press my hands over my ears. From the first quavering notes, I can feel again how everything has changed. The city streets below aren't the same streets as a few hours ago. The cardboard box behind the Chinese restaurant isn't the same cardboard box. There is blood smeared on my lips, and I let it remain.

■ ■ ■ ■ ■

The graffiti appears several days later. Or maybe it's been there all along. The back walls of the Chinese restaurant are covered with slogans and scribbles, but this morning one particular tag catches my eye. It's a silver spray paint sketch of a king's crown with a line through it. A single word is scrawled underneath. It says "Seen." I sit in my cardboard box and fixate on it for several minutes. I'm entranced by the flowing and interlocking lines of the design. They leave me with an inexplicable chill.

My thoughts are interrupted by the sound of chorgling noises from the nearby dumpster. The fat kid must be back again. His head shoots up above the metal rim, his face smeared with the runny leftovers of General Tsao's Chicken and Egg Foo Young. He's worse than the rats. He gorges himself on almost everything, including the greased plastic paper. I scoop some loose rocks and bottle caps off the ground and hurl them at him. "Get out of here," I hiss.

It's the only way to get his attention. The fat kid is virtually a zombie. His eyes are dead, as if any spark of personality has been buried beneath an avalanche of bad fortune. He lets out a pathetic bleat and clambers up the fire escape, vanishing onto a nearby roof. Typically, the only edibles he's left in the dumpster are the remains of the oranges the restaurant serves with its fortune cookies. I collect several slices and stuff them into my pockets. I pat my sweatshirt to make sure the tape player and my cassette are still there. It's time to find some real food.

Walking the streets, on the lookout for any of the scattered Luchos, I spot several more silver tags. They materialize in out-of-the-way places: The lip of a mailbox, the back of a crosswalk sign, the inner curb of a sidewalk. At first, I figure they must be different from the graffiti on the wall. But the design is always the same. The crossed-out king's crown. The word "Seen." Nobody else seems to pay much attention to this graffiti.

Now that they're on my radar, the tags appear everywhere. They blanket the row of abandoned buildings near the park. They're scrawled over kicked-in doorways, next to corroded fire escapes, across boarded-up windows. They bloom on ravaged walls and overflowing trash cans. An enormous silver crown glints off the bus shelter for the crosstown local. I run my fingers along its lines and trace the contours, trying to read some message in the tack and texture of the paint.

My body starts to shiver. There's a subterranean surge of excitement as I remove the tape case from my sweatshirt and place it next to the graffiti. After a careful comparison of the handwriting, there's no doubt: The person who painted these is the same one who left me the cassette.

I want to believe these tags are encrypted personal messages. They're puzzles to solve. They're an invitation whose time is running out. I need some space to deliberate, so I hop the nearby fence and wander through the park. I select an empty wooden bench near the playground. I suck on several orange rinds while I try to untangle my thoughts.

I find myself staring at a nearby lamppost. There's another tag but this one looks different. Maybe it's a trick of the light, but the image of the crossed-out crown seems to shimmer. I kneel on the asphalt to study it up close. My fingers trace the curves of the design. It has a slippery feel. The tag appears smeared and I can't figure out why until I look down at my hands. The paint is still wet.

The person must be nearby. I spring to my feet and begin to search the park. Everyone around me becomes a suspect: The dog-walker with three lunging hounds on a single leash; the heavy-lidded woman whose shopping bags encircle her feet; the bum with the rabbinical beard and newspaper shoes who greets passersby with kissing noises.

I exit the park and madly scan the streets. My mind buzzes like a burning beehive. I'm looking for anyone smuggling a can of spray paint. I scrutinize the shifty-eyed punk sprawled in a doorway with his shoplifted cans of warm beer. The Hispanic man perched in front of the bodega, massaging the batteries of his busted cell phone. The drag queen who touches up her rouge while waiting for the express bus. Their blank expressions don't give anything away. Maybe they're not part of this game.

I scour the neighborhood, methodically threading my way through the grid of streets and occasionally zigzagging headlong down one of the avenues, but I don't have any luck and eventually return to my base. When I reach the Chinese restaurant, a pony-tailed Asian waitress is stationed next to the nearby pay phone, chain-smoking a pack of unfiltered cigarettes. It looks like she's about to say something to me when the phone rings.

She places her hand over the receiver in a proprietary way but doesn't pick it up. While I wait for this curious drama to play out, I stare into the window of the restaurant. A trio of teenagers are huddled around a pot of tea and an order of steamed dumplings. Their fingers are coated in silver spray paint.

I peek my head inside. These two boys and the girl are the only customers in the dingy dining room. They seem lost in heady conversation. A cardboard stencil is propped next to the girl's tea cup. It's a king's crown with a line through it. As I ease myself inside, the metal prayer bell tied to the door handle gives a harsh jingle. The trio spins around.

I stumble a few steps toward them. My mind stammers. I'm dumbstruck, or terrified, or maybe just overexcited. No emotion stands still long enough to name. I have no idea how to explain myself, so I remove the plastic tape case from my sweatshirt and hold it out. By way of introduction.

The trio silently consults one another, then motions me over to their booth. None of them seems surprised by my presence. "We were wondering when we'd run into you," the girl says.

Looking at them sitting here, next to a fish tank filled with stunted carp and surrounded by strains of pinched Eastern folk music, something occurs to me. The obviousness and enormity of it buckles my knees. In a hushed and imploring voice, I ask: "Did you make the music on this tape?"

It's impossible to read the contorted shapes their faces make, the cryptic crisscrosses of furrowed brows and creased lips. They look like I've just complimented their dead mother's ass. The girl finally speaks up. "That's not us," she says. "The singer on that tape is Kin Mersey."

The trio introduce themselves. The girl calls herself Lena. Her hair is a tangle of red, yellow, and black ringlets, the roots of previous dye jobs aggressively on display. The ratty locks almost seem like an apology for her delicate and classically beautiful features. The boy caressing the back of her neck is Hank. He flashes a high-wattage grin. His bare arms are covered in elaborately primitive designs, but these interlocking totems resemble magic marker scrawls more than actual tattoos. I try not to stare at the other boy whose disfigured profile seems to be the result of a terrible burn. Markus has sparkling eyes that belie his taciturn expression. He slides over to make room for me in their booth.

Lena takes out a wallet constructed of black duct tape and extracts a photograph that's been folded into eight equal-sized squares. She arranges the image in front of me. "This is Kin," she explains.

It's a grainy shot of a small rock club. There are low ceilings, black curtains tacked against the walls, a set of speakers dangling above the wooden stage. Several pasty guys play an assortment of drums, trumpets, dismantled synthesizers, and cable patches. But the focus is on the lead singer with his frizzy blond curls and a red scarf wrapped around his squat neck. This has to be Kin Mersey—his mouth open wide and his teeth bared. He's captured mid-yawp. He coddles a battered acoustic guitar in the crook of his arms like a sleeping infant and appears utterly lost in the undertow of the song.

"This is from his final show," Markus says. "It's the last confirmed picture of him."

"He quit in the middle of the tour," Hank adds. "He sold all his instruments on a street corner and vanished. Nobody has seen him in years."

I examine the photo more closely, as if it's one of those optical paintings where you adjust your focus and an embedded image suddenly emerges. There is something unsettling about the way Kin seems so absorbed in the moment, his eyes as white as boiled eggs, rolled back into their sockets.

"Why'd he quit?" I ask.

"Nobody knows," Lena says. She takes a long sip of tea and

swallows hard. I notice the dusting of silver spray paint on her knuckles and the base of the cup.

"I saw the graffiti," I say. "I wasn't sure what it meant."

Lena flips over the photograph of Kin Mersey. On the backside, there's a smaller image of Kin sitting on a stoop wearing a paper crown on his head. It's rakishly askew. He probably got it from a fast food restaurant but it still manages to look defiantly regal. "The crown is his symbol," she explains. "It started as some inside joke, but the image stuck." As she talks, her hand obsessively traces and retraces the image. "There are rumors Kin is hiding out in one of the nearby projects. We did the tags to get his attention. To coax him out into the open." She straightens the collar of her immaculately tattered raincoat. "That's also why I gave you the tape."

"But why me?"

"You're on the street," Lena says. "You know what's really happening." She sweeps aside her multi-colored tresses so there's nothing obscuring her eyes. "You must have heard some stories about Kin. You have to know something."

Her challenging tone and imploring look make this feel like a test. Though it's pretty obvious I don't know a thing, there still seems to be a correct response. I close my eyes and recall Kin's unearthly voice.

"Maybe he hasn't quit," I say. "Maybe he's making music in secret. Maybe he's waiting for people to catch up to his new sounds."

There's a stretch of silence where the only sounds are the clank of utensils in the kitchen and the murmur of foreign dialects. Then Lena smiles. She says to her friends: "I told you he was all right."

Lena pours some tea into a chipped china cup and hands it to me. It's a clear liquid that turns out to be pure grain alcohol. I cough after the first burning swallow.

Markus laughs and pats me on the back. "We love the tea

here," he says. "It's their specialty. You'll get a taste for it pretty quick."

Hank remains silent. He still seems to be evaluating me. His arms are crossed and his thumb circles one of the black totems on his bicep. His gaze remains trained on me. "Before we get all cozy," he says, "we need you to do something for us."

Hank looks pointedly at Lena. She nods and fishes in the inner pocket of her overcoat. She places a runny can of silver spray paint on the table, then slides the cardboard stencil next to it. Lastly, she produces a cassette from her bag that looks strikingly similar to mine. She gives me a shrug that seems apologetic, almost.

Hank says: "Paint some tags around the neighborhood to help us spread the word."

He says: "Give the tape to someone who might have information about Kin and see what you can find out."

He says: "Once you've done that, come find us."

Hank rolls up the sleeve of my sweatshirt and writes a street address on my forearm in black felt-tip marker. Then he throws a few crumpled bills on the table and leads the others out of the restaurant. Lena waves to me over her shoulder. "Hope to see you soon," she says. I watch as the door swings shut behind them. The bell tied to the handle clangs several times and the sound echoes through the empty dining room, rippling in waves that take a long time to dissipate.

I sit alone in the booth, scarfing down the leftover dumplings and emptying the teapot. My mind slowly grapples with the tasks I've been assigned. I absently scrape the silver paint from the nozzle of the spray can while strategizing the most effective placement for graffiti and ideal candidates for the cassette. There are so many variables that my head spins. Eventually I decide the best solution is to complete my charge as soon as possible. Spray a few desultory tags across the neighborhood. Give the tape to the first person I see.

When I leave the restaurant, my sweatshirt bulges with the tools of my mission. Almost immediately, I spot the Asian waitress. She's now talking on the pay phone, the plastic receiver cupped in the crook of her neck. She speaks in a terse code punctuated by stabbing and balletic hand gestures. It doesn't sound like English and given the hushed quality of her voice, it could just as easily be an invented private language.

I decide to wait for her and duck into the alleyway. I kill time by experimenting with the stencil and spraying the design onto the back of a nearby air conditioning unit. It takes several tries to get it right. I freestyle the last part and underneath write the word "Unseen." I'm admiring my handiwork when there's a scuttle of overturning trash and toppling boxes. At first, it sounds like a pack of ravenous rats. But then I realize it's the perfect solution.

I walk silently toward the metal dumpster on the balls of my feet. I switch the cassette excitedly from hand to hand. It feels heavier than usual. I recall its potential to open up new vistas and alter the fabric of the recipient's dreams. And here is someone who truly needs it.

The fat kid's head pops over the rim of the dumpster. He must recognize me but the unformed expression on his face doesn't give anything away. His eyes are mere holes. His blotchy skin is pasty and puffy. His cheeks are full of food that he mechanically continues to chew.

I hold out the cassette in the palm of my hand. I smile and inch closer, moving with calm deliberation, the way you'd approach a skittish doe, trying not to spook him. The slightest ember of light glints behind his dead eyes. He seems intrigued. "Don't be scared," I coax. "This is a gift."

I have faith this simple gesture will be understood. The traffic behind me sounds like a guitar being tuned up, a discordant series of notes that's preparing to resolve into something glorious. I move a few steps closer. I keep my palm perfectly flat. "It's a tape," I say. "It's for you."

He seems to comprehend. He tentatively reaches out his stubby fingers and snatches it from me. He sniffs the edges of the plastic case and kneads it with his hands. Then he removes the cassette and raises its shiny black shell to the sunlight for closer inspection. He stares at it with a sense of wonder, as if he spies another world in there among all that tape. Maybe he's more like me than I thought. This is how I must have looked when I first received this music. "Thank you," he says in a slurred voice.

I remove the walkman from the folds of my sweatshirt. But before I can hand it to him, he pops the cassette into his mouth and cracks it between his teeth. As he begins to chew, bits of unspooled magnetic tape curl between his lips, but somehow he manages to swallow. He pats his stomach. His beaming cheeks form a grin. His shiny eyes well up with tears of gratitude.

■ ■ ■ ■ ■

I stand in front of the window, hypnotized. There I am staring back at myself staring at the arrangement of green Gretsch guitar, white drum kit, black enamel bass. The instruments look like they're floating on top of my body. One reality superimposed over the other. I'm flanked by Markus and Lena who seem to be experiencing the same thing. It's like a hallucination, or maybe a vision. The three of us must all be thinking something similar but I'm the one who says it, half-whispering the words under my breath because the idea is so potent that anything louder would shatter the glass: "We look like a band."

There's no point entering the store to inquire about prices. The place is so new it hasn't officially opened for business, but more importantly we're flat broke. We peel ourselves away from the display window, hijacked by a snarl of conflicting emotions.

My words have clearly initiated something. As we walk back to the squat, we argue about who would play what instrument. Markus immediately claims guitar for himself. Lena shouts drums like she's calling shotgun. I finger the shell necklace around my throat. "I don't care," I say. "As long as I get to sing." They raise their eyebrows in concert, but I'm pretty sure I could do it.

When we reach the deteriorating tenement, we linger on the street until the homeless couple turns the corner, then scurry down the steps to the basement. The kids call this "the squat," but it's an actual apartment Lena inherited from some relative or another. She removes the key pinned inside her eloquently distressed wool sweater and unlocks the door.

I've been crashing with them for several months, but this place hasn't lost its novelty. The sprawling, raw space is furnished with a few rickety chairs, soiled mattresses, and corked piss bottles. Food wrappers carpet the cracked concrete floor. Black tapestries annul the windows. It's modest but there's electricity and running water. And even better, a booming stereo system. We're about to announce the discovery of the music store when the sound blasting from the speakers stops us.

The muffled ferocity is immediately identifiable. It's the bootleg cassette of Kin Mersey's final show. This particular recording is almost never played. In the time I've been here, the kids have only dared to break it out once. Hank sits on the mattress he shares with Lena, wrapped in their stained sheets, hugging his knees. It almost looks like he's been crying. We've clearly arrived in the aftermath of something.

The walls rattle from the sound of the band ratcheting up for another headlong chorus. The tape is striking for its scrim of fuzz and static, but one element is instantly clear. That voice. The performance contains no obvious clues to Kin's sudden abdication though it's marked by an intensity that's eerie even by his extreme standards, a disturbing vodoun vibe where it's impossible to tell whether he is channeling the songs, or vice versa. Hank starts to stir. He says: "There's something you guys need to see."

As Hank stands up, I notice his fingertips are smudged black. In a few places, the ink from the interwoven patterns on his arms is beginning to run. He solemnly presents us with a blurred photocopy of what looks like an X-ray. There's some scratchy handwriting below the image and a sequence of typed numbers. It appears to be the cross-section of a human skull, its mouth wide open. There is a square chunk of bright matter behind the teeth. "A friend of mine works in the psych ward and was there when it happened," Hank says. "He figured we'd want to know and snuck me this copy."

"I don't get it," Lena says. "What exactly are we looking at?"

"A severed tongue," he says. "Apparently Kin chewed off his own tongue during like the tenth round of electroshock therapy."

We silently pass the image from hand to hand. Holding the page, I'm visited by a feeling similar to the one I had staring at the store window. My collar bone thrums and my stomach flops.

Hank tacks the paper to the wall, where it hangs like some kind of fucked-up talisman. The copy is too smudged to tell anything for certain—even the name on the X-ray isn't conclusive, the scratchy doctor handwriting typically illegible. But this seems beside the point. Hank's tale sounds grotesque enough to be true. There have been persistent rumors that Kin suffers from schizophrenic episodes.

Everyone is devastated. Markus tries to buoy us with logic and lamely plays devil's advocate. "There have been all sorts of crazy stories about Kin," he says. "Who says this one has to be true?" Hank says his friend isn't a liar and points out that none of the previous rumors have been backed up by hard evidence. I try to add my two cents, but no words come out. It falls to Lena to supply the verdict. "It's depressing," she says. "Really fucking depressing." The tape winds past the final number and now only scattered shards of murmurs and applause emanate from the speakers, the sound of the audience making its way toward the exits.

When the stereo clicks off, the silence is jarring. I find my index finger hypnotically tracing the outline of the X-ray as if it formed a sort of map, as if it were a pattern to be brought into focus. Then I have it.

I say: "The new music store in the neighborhood."

I say: "It's only a few blocks from here."

I say: "We're going to steal the instruments."

As soon as the words come out, I know they're exactly right. Markus nods in agreement. Hank seems unsure at first, but slowly a smile emerges. "It's beyond perfect," Lena says. "We'll carry on Kin's music for him."

Hank takes the lead in masterminding a plan. It should be straightforward, but he wants to know about more than the store's location and the instruments in the window. He obsesses over the likely floor plan, the possible security system, the layout of the primary street and surrounding avenues. Strategies are hatched about disabling alarm mechanisms, spray-painting the lenses of security cameras, establishing the quickest routes of entry and escape. "This is impossible without a van," Hank says. I roll my eyes, but it turns out Lena knows someone who can lend us one. Markus alone has second thoughts. It's difficult to read the level of concern in his burned features, but he keeps hinting at misgivings about the morality of the proposition.

Lena defends the idea as my brainchild. "This is the way people on the street get things done," she says.

"It's a basic right," I clarify. "Like starving people who steal bread."

Hank puts a slightly different spin on it. "Come on," he says. "Anybody stupid enough to open a music store in such a shitty neighborhood deserves this."

The planning continues for what feels like hours. Maybe it's a necessary part of screwing up our courage. That evening we're finally ready to make a dry run and fine-tune the details of our heist. We borrow a beat-up white van that looks well acquainted with this line of work. Hank rolls up the schematic drawings he's concocted and announces he'll drive. Markus, Lena, and I huddle on the metal floor in the back. It feels like we're apostles on our first mission. Markus hums the riff to a favorite Kin Mersey song, Lena taps out the beat on her stomach, and I imagine my voice soaring over top of it all.

We park the van a block away and casually saunter toward the music store. It's one of the few occupied storefronts in this so-called commercial zone of the neighborhood. Even in the hazy light of the sporadic streetlamps, I can tell something is wrong. The display window looks unreal, as if it's mystically shed one of its dimensions. Then I notice a shimmer of glass on the sidewalk and realize we're too late. It's been smashed. As we creep closer, I spot a metal trash can lying inside the store. Some bastard tossed it through the glass and cleaned out the instruments. We hear police sirens approaching and tear back to the van. We haven't done anything wrong but Hank peels maniacally around random corners until the sound dies away. Eventually we shudder to a stop outside a bar, somewhere on the far edge of our neighborhood.

The bar is open, so we're forced to get drunk. We slump into a table and order several rounds simultaneously. "This is just a setback," Hank says. "We're still going to do this. There's no doubt about it." But I can feel the momentum draining away. Our platitudes about carrying on sound listless, like speeches at an infant's wake. We try to distract ourselves by focusing on the band that's getting ready to play on the wooden stage in the corner.

Lena has an idea. She smoothes her multi-color tresses, fixes her lipstick, pastes on her cutest smile, and strolls over to request a number by Kin Mersey. A balm for our disappointments. She returns to the table wearing a potent scowl. "They've never heard of him," she says, spitting on the floor. It figures. The band of athletic longhair dudes start to bang out some third-hand hard rock. The longer we listen, the clearer it becomes these so-called musicians are committing crimes against art. The sight of them playing these instruments makes as much sense as Neanderthals operating sonar.

We outwait the band as a matter of principle. After their interminable set, I notice them dragging their equipment through a service entrance into the street. I pretend to use the bathroom so I can get a better view. I watch them carefully arrange the drum kit and bass amps in the back of a van. I rush back inside, grip the side of the table so hard the beer bottles rattle, and let it blurt.

I say: "There's a van outside full of instruments."

I say: "Stealing them from these assholes will be a favor to society."

I say: "We've got to hurry."

We sketch a quick plan and arrive on the scene just in time. The band is loitering on the sidewalk. Their van is loaded with the instruments. Hank waves his arms and calls out to them, launching into his crazed fan routine. "You guys rock!" he says. He somehow keeps a straight face while asking if they have albums for sale and when they've got their next gig. Of course the band has neither, but they talk a good game about future plans. Even the driver climbs out of the front seat to explain that they've been thinking about changing their name and rattles off some idiotic options they've been considering. Hank asks for their autographs and when nobody has paper, he hoists his shirt and insists they sign his stomach.

Oh, it's pathetically easy. Markus, Lena, and I casually sneak around the other side of the van. Markus is prepared to attempt a fast hotwire, but the driver has left the keys on the seat. We pile inside, lock the side doors, and Markus guns the ignition. The engine turns over with a wheezing gasp. The van rattles and we take off with a shuddering jolt. As we lurch down the street, I see the lead singer running down the sidewalk after us, blond hair cascading behind him, arms and legs pumping furiously. But it hardly matters. There's nothing but clear road ahead.

Then the engine stalls. Markus jockeys the key and the van frantically restarts. We look up to find the lead singer has thrown his body against the hood, his fleshy fingers clutching the windshield wipers. His lanky hair conceals his eyes but his contorted lips and crooked teeth form a terrifying grimace. "You're gonna have to run me over," he shouts.

"Do it," Lena screams. Markus hits the gas and the guy spins off the windshield like a giant pinwheel. It's sort of alarming. The instruments buckle and the rear doors fly open. The bass and several amps tumble into the street with a series of rumbling thumps. In the rearview, Hank is getting pummeled by several band members who look like they're blending his face into the pavement.

The engine finally catches the correct gear and the speedometer leaps upward. But two blocks later, we hit a red light. Three sedans and an SUV are stopped ahead of us. Markus leans on the horn, but nobody budges. "This fucking traffic," he groans. I look behind to see the lead singer shambling down the center of the street. His face is bloody. He's picked up the bass from the asphalt and wields it like a baseball bat. He flails the air and unleashes a series of inarticulate shrieks.

"For God's sake," I shout. "Run it!"

"In case you haven't noticed," Markus begins, but then looks over his shoulder. As we peel out, the singer swings the bass at the flapping back doors and almost knocks one off its hinges. We sweep around the stopped cars and Markus briefly shuts his eyes as we careen down the wrong side of the street. He runs the next several lights for insurance, then initiates a sequence of random turns, mimicking Hank's getaway technique. A few more amps topple out of the rear of the van. None of us has any idea where we're heading.

After all the moving violations and falling equipment, it's no surprise to see the police's flashing red lights in the rearview mirror. "Keep going," I shout. Markus floors the accelerator and makes several swerving turns, shunting over sidewalks and mowing down trash cans. All of a sudden he hits the brakes so hard that we bounce off the windshield. We've reached the end of a cul-de-sac, one of the many streets that terminates at the canal. We stumble out of the van, dazed and winded, clutching our heads while executing a few looping steps. I hear a siren in the distance but the police aren't in sight yet.

Before fleeing the scene, we rifle through the shambling heap of equipment. Markus seizes a scuffed guitar; Lena nabs a snare drum; my fingers find themselves coiled around a microphone cable. We unsteadily hop the guardrail at the end of the road and take off down the concrete bank of the canal. The squeal of braking tires and relayed calls of stern voices let us know the cops have found the van.

We run single-file along the lip of the canal. Our bodies huff and pant, but the adrenaline courses through our limbs and soon we fall into a steady cadence. We ignore the approaching shouts and roving flashlight beams. The path ahead seems clear. A canopy of intermittent stars provides the main illumination and the glassy surface of the canal throws our reflections back at us. It looks like we're running upside-down, the soles of our shoes skimming the top of the water.

I tune in to the snare clanging against Lena's hips like a tambourine. It suggests the martial pulse of the song we'd hummed earlier. Between breaths, Markus starts to vocalize the main guitar riff. I swallow hard, then launch into the lyrics. I'm out of breath and scared shitless, but that must help because it doesn't sound half bad. We maintain our pace, repeating the surging chorus in our halting manner, over and over. Behind us, we can make out the rhythm of running footsteps and jangling handcuffs. There is also the faint but distinct humming of several voices. The police, who are getting closer, have picked up the song.

■ ■ ■ ■ ■

He doesn't seem to realize I've been following him for blocks. The man purposefully winds his way through the midday crowds without a backward glance. That's him up ahead in the mottled gray terrycloth bathrobe, the red scarf, the black canvas high-top sneakers. He obsessively shakes his frizzy blond curls out of his eyes and scratches at his cheeks. The other pedestrians probably write him off as a freak, another psychotic vagrant who wandered into his own head and promptly lost the compass. The city is littered with these sorts of casualties. But I suspect this man is something else.

Every few paces, I have to break into a jog to keep him in my sights. The man acts like he's late for an appointment. He speeds past the shuttered laundromats, the half-empty junk shops, the buckling brick apartment buildings with grime-frosted windows. His reflection never pauses long enough to register my stare. I've been following him since he first brushed past me on the sidewalk, hanging behind at a watchful distance, afraid to miss anything.

The man steps off the sidewalk mid-block and bounds across the street, oblivious to the horns of oncoming traffic. A taxi swerves over the dividing line to avoid hitting him. Squealing brakes, shouted curses, a choir of middle-fingers. It's a choreographed melee of sound and steel that the man absently conducts as he passes through like an apparition. Time seems to stretch, though his journey to the opposite sidewalk probably only takes a few seconds. Before I can blink twice, he's vanished into the park.

I dash across the street, but the man is nowhere to be seen. The entrance to the park brims with the usual shuffling armada of runaways with stolen skateboards, homeless with borrowed shopping carts, police practicing blindness behind their shades. On a hunch, I follow the route that winds along the park's perimeter. The sun shimmers off the concrete and the oaks overhead are too exhausted to supply a full canopy, so I have to keep squinting. I spot him in the distance, arms swinging briskly at his side, as if his shadow is a prison he's determined to outrun.

Somebody calls my name. I spot Hank and Lena cuddled on a nearby wooden bench, waving me over. I nod but keep walking. No time for niceties. The man appears to be heading for the exit by the steel band shell and I can't risk losing him. I hear my name again and soon am flanked on either side by my friends.

"Impressively rude," Hank says. "What's the story?"

"Sorry." I speak without breaking my stride. "I'm following somebody."

"Intrigue," says Hank. "I like it."

"See that guy up there?" I'm careful not to be so flagrant as to actually point. "The one in the gray bathrobe?" There's nothing to do but blurt it out. "I think that's Kin Mersey."

There's a silence, then Lena says: "Oh my God."

The man leaves the park and immediately tacks east, heading deeper into the shittiest streets of this shitty neighborhood. The three of us follow in a state of entranced speechlessness. It's only now that we notice the lack of silver tags from our graffiti campaign. In their place are rows of unconscious homeless men curled atop cardboard pallets, their gray beards flecked with bits of newspaper. Stray dogs lick discarded alkaline batteries, looking for a leftover charge. The air is perfumed with stale urine and rancid government cheese.

As we walk, I shuffle through the endless unconfirmed

stories about Kin Mersey in my mind. There's only one rumor that truly interests me. It claims Kin has feverishly continued to write songs, generating tunes shot through with shards of terrifying beauty, creating music so radical that even his fans aren't ready to hear it.

The storefronts start to thin out, but the man doesn't seem to register the change. Soon it's strictly rubble-strewn lots, half-demolished concrete foundations, construction fences slotted with suggestive gaps. He pauses at a traffic light to cinch the bathrobe tighter, keeping the terrycloth from flapping in the updrafts from passing vehicles. We cluster around a telephone pole, pretending to be fascinated by a handwritten notice about a missing hamster. This is the closest I've been to the man since he first passed me. My heart hammers in the slender vein dividing my forehead.

"You really think it's Kin?" Hank whispers.

"It does sort of look like him," Lena says.

The man's face is swollen. His hands are chafed and raw. But the resemblance is clear. A red scarf is wrapped around the same squat neck that you'd never believe could house such an unearthly voice. The same unkempt blond hair, the same gangly frame, the same pupils drowning in that peculiar shade of cerulean blue. The words buzz in my mouth as I speak them. "It's him."

The man races onward. We automatically fall in behind. The crosstown expressway looms ahead, emitting a high-pitched rumble, the singing sound of rubber tires on asphalt. Several metal shopping carts lie gutted on the pavement like they've been gang-raped. Blackbirds squat on the telephone wires, chirping intricate tunes no one can hear. By now it's obvious we're tailing the guy. We're the only figures in this desolate landscape. The man doesn't acknowledge our presence, but my senses tingle with an animal suspicion that he knows we're here.

His pace quickens. The air crackles with nervous energy as

we realize he must be close to his final destination. High-rise apartment towers appear in the distance. Grids of identical rectangular balconies teem with makeshift clotheslines. The pinned sheets, shirts, and socks flap in the wind like flags. Ornate letters writ large in Krylon transform the sides of buildings into concrete pages from a vast illuminated manuscript. Flashes of technicolor graffiti signify cryptic warnings. He's leading us into the heart of the projects.

"Maybe the rumors about him living here are true," Lena says. She throws me a cautious smile. "I knew you'd lead us to him."

All at once, we're not alone. Sullen Haitian boys encircle a broken pay phone, their feet batting the dangling receiver like a tetherball. A trio of slit-eyed Dominican teenage girls lean against a rusted mailbox and pick their teeth. A tattooed bodega owner dumps a bucket of dirty water on the curb. We collect a catalog of suspicious and hostile stares. The three of us fall progressively farther back, afraid the man is going to get jumped and beaten, afraid the same thing might happen to us.

The man approaches the largest apartment tower. He walks past the drained cement fountain and into the empty courtyard. He pauses on one of the few green patches left in the expanse of dried mud and shriveled shrubs. He scoops up a handful of dirt and gravel and tosses it at the building. A few of the pebbles reach the third floor. This seems to be some sort of signal. In the surrounding windows, the curtains part and sets of wrinkled faces materialize from the shadows. We form another set of curious eyes on the periphery, the three of us crouched behind a dumpster.

While the man waits, he paws the ground with his worn sneakers, like a dressage horse before a demanding routine. He bends down to scoop up another handful of something, then stands motionless except for a vigorous movement of the teeth. It takes a moment to understand that he's chewing a mouthful of grass. Green stalks and stems protrude from his lips.

"Fucking A," Hank says. "He's totally lost it."

"Poor thing," Lena says. "Maybe he's getting in touch with his primal side. Sometimes that's the creative way to deal with pain."

"Maybe it soothes his throat," I offer.

"Come on," Hank says. "He's just another fuck-up now. He's a dude with no tongue, wearing a bathrobe, chewing on grass."

"Him chewing off his tongue was a rumor," I say. "We still don't know if that really happened."

"Take a look at the guy," Hank says. "That's all I'm saying."

But I don't see him that way. I half-recall tales about Old Testament prophets stabling themselves in meadows and devouring handfuls of grass as part of vision quests. Perhaps this is also part of some unseen process, a sort of metamorphosis, a peculiar demand of his muse.

There's movement in one of the upper windows. The systematic blinking of a curtain, maybe. It happens, but the man clearly discerns the signal and approaches the entrance of the building. Before he can press the buzzer, the glass doors burst open and he's ambushed by a shrill tribe of children. They poke and prod him, venture close then leap back with delighted cries. A chubby black girl with cornrows lets out a piercing shriek and all the kids laugh like it's some kind of punch line. A solemn raven-haired girl holds the door open and offers the man her upturned hand. He gently clasps it and allows himself to be led inside, the whooping kids trailing behind.

Hank and Lena look uneasy, but we've got to move if we don't want to lose him. We reach the lobby in time to spot the tail-end of the children's procession winding its way into a concrete stairwell. The gang of kids stomp up the stairs, pleased by the resounding echo of their own footsteps. Their destination seems to be a couple of flights overhead. The man must be in the lead.

We trail them to the third floor. The long hallway is dimly lit. The ambient gurgle of breakbeat salsa and game-show reruns filter through the walls. The children are gathered outside an apartment whose door is ajar, spilling a parallelogram of light onto the linoleum tiles. Just as we realize that the man must be already inside, the door swings shut.

The children's chattering draws the attention of the floor's residents. A few curious heads appear in the hall to investigate. Soon there's a loose queue of adults and children outside the closed door. We hug the wall and try to pass for a natural part of this crowd. Lena flattens her hair to downplay the flamboyant purple streaks. Hank rolls down his sleeves to obscure the ever stranger ink patterns. I pull up the hood of my sweatshirt and disappear inside the cowl.

The apartment opens. A tall man in a shiny black ski jacket and hand-me-down grimace lets people inside. This must have already happened a few times because there's an unspoken protocol. Everyone drops their shoes in the hallway before filing inside. We enter a modest living room with white pressboard walls and industrial gray carpeting. There's no sign of the man. The blinds are drawn and fluorescent lights bathe everything in an antiseptic blue. The place is undecorated except for a single oil painting: A nude Amazon with a large afro reclines on a tiger-skin rug. Her ankles are shackled but her curled lips form a defiant sneer. One hand hoists a barbed iron spear heavenward and the other strokes the pink folds of her labia.

The place soon fills up. A mix of old men, pimply teenagers, and mothers hauling infants straggle in behind us. We find an open space on the floor and sit cross-legged. I'm starting to feel like an idiot. I'm only wearing socks on my feet and sitting in a strange apartment in the projects. The solemn girl with black hair stares directly at us. The other children glower and giggle. They elongate their cheeks and pick their noses. Their eyes sparkle like phosphorescence.

A women in curlers turns to me: "You here for the show?"

I must look confused because she points to the empty twin

bed pressed against the far wall. It functions as a couch. Or maybe a stage. But here's the important detail: A child's plaything lies atop the bare mattress. I've been staring at it but not really seeing it. My brain has balked because the implications are too startling. My breathing becomes shallow. My mind spirals. I sense Hank and Lena also struggling to process the sight. "Here comes the something," Lena whispers, from a favorite lyric. The object on the bed is a miniature guitar.

"Don't get too excited," Hank tells us. "It's only a toy." But the tone of his voice betrays the fact that his expectations have been raised as well.

There's the sound of activity in the hallway behind us. A man in a red track suit makes an entrance. His coffee-colored skin and regal features are offset by a flat nose that appears to have been broken numerous times. A few hushed murmurs of a name: "Morrisot." He gracefully navigates the room, tousling kids' hair and shaking a few hands. His cleared throat resounds like trumpet fanfare.

"Welcome," Morrisot says in a rich baritone. "A friend of mine is going to provide entertainment for us this afternoon. He's a bit unusual, but don't be alarmed. He'll do whatever I say." He signals the man in the black ski jacket to flip off the overhead fluorescents and turn on the bedside lamp. Mood lighting. He produces a small plastic packet of yellowish powder from his sweatshirt. He shakes the packet briskly between thumb and forefinger. The sort of precise gesture aristocrats use to ring a service bell.

The man we've been following lopes to the edge of the room, rubbing his gums and flashing a hideous grin at no one in particular. The way his eyes are locked on the plastic packet, the rest of the apartment might as well be empty. Morrisot tries to coax him deeper into the room but the man sticks with the shadows. He refuses the bait for several moments, then lunges for the packet. Like a matador working with a tiny cape, Morrisot flicks it out of reach and the man crashes headfirst into the bed. The crowd offers murmurs of approval.

Morrisot helps the man to his feet and smoothes his tangled bathrobe. He speaks to him in a voice that's soft but firm, precisely enunciating each word so there's no misunderstanding. "You want some," Morrisot says, "then you have to play us a song." He nestles the pint-sized guitar into the man's hands.

The man unwinds his red scarf, sheds his bathrobe, and faces the crowd. It's Kin Mersey. There's no mistaking him. Only Lena seems unfazed by his extravagant deterioration. There's an arctic paleness to his flesh. You can map the blue veins coursing throughout his bare chest. His face is scarred with pink pustules. His eyes are yellow and liverish. His teeth are rotted. The cuticle of every nail has been gnawed past the quick. My heart sinks, but then Kin licks his lips. You can clearly see the tip of a full crimson tongue.

Morrisot whispers something in Kin's ear, coaxing him the way you'd handle a skittish show pony. It's suddenly as if he's more of a manager than a dealer, and it occurs to me that we may be about to hear a preview of the new sounds Kin has been working on.

Kin tentatively touches the frets of the guitar. A preternatural alertness has crept into his expression. Kin's slender fingers tremble as they adjust the tines, but they approximate a sound that's in tune. Lena squeezes Hank's hands and mine. None of us is prepared for what may be about to happen. I shake myself loose from the circuit. I have to experience this for myself.

As Kin starts to strum, I'm surprised by the volume that ripples from the toy instrument. He beats out a rhythm that replicates the headlong urgency of his steps. At first the chords seem to coalesce into a familiar song, but then they violently fracture, suggesting something entirely new. My body begins to ignite. Kin leans into the rapidly splintering sound but can't seem to find his entrance, as if the words are locked in his windpipe.

His lips foam and quiver. His eyes swing back in their sockets. Sweat crowns his forehead. When he finally opens his mouth, he unleashes a terrible howl.

The sound comes choking out in convulsive yelps. The children burst into peals of hysterical laughter. This is the punch line they've been awaiting, but it's no joke. A tormented expression strangles Kin Mersey's features. He begins to weep while continuing to play. Drool collects around the edges of his lips. There's a tragic, desperate intimacy to the performance. It's so overwhelming that I shut my eyes. I can't face Hank's knowing contempt or Lena's romanticized rapture. Everything around me feels like it's turning to ash.

Kin lets loose another round of high-pitched shrieks. I have to get out of here. I abandon my friends, push past the crowd, and scramble through the hallway in stocking feet. I bound down the stairs three at a time, trying to forget about the spittle massing around Kin's mouth, not waiting to discover the fate of that one still expanding bubble of saliva.

CHAPTER 5
MY LIFE IN EXILE
(15 years old)

"What will we do to disappear?"
−Maurice Blanchot

I'M NOT PAYING ATTENTION TO TRAFFIC SIGNALS. My gaze is trained on my rotting sneakers. I'm in a half-zombie state, shuffling across the street wherever I feel like it. Let them honk if they're about to hit me.

Not that there are many people out on this gray Sunday morning. I can't remember exactly where I'm wandering. It's one of those indistinguishable neighborhoods on the outskirts of the city. The blank modern façades try hard to appear antiseptic but the structural rot peeks through even the freshest coats of paint. The narrow streets are empty except for a lone figure dressed in molting clothes and cradling a bandaged hand. That's me. I'm prospecting for a promising corner to collect change for a bus ticket. The final destination doesn't matter. I just want to be in a different city. I'm too hollowed out to be picky.

I'm heading through the intersection of the main boulevard when something tugs at my shirt. A man yanks me back onto the curb. He immediately apologizes, speaking in a foreign-inflected English. "I am so sorry," he says, looking genuinely aggrieved. I figure a truck must have been careening toward us, but the street is empty. There's not even any slow-circling taxis, chumming for fares. "I am so sorry you're sick," the man continues. "It is painful for me because a dear friend of mine had the same disease. This is a terrible thing to see a young person in such a state."

I have no idea what he's talking about. Maybe there's a glitch in the translation of his thoughts. "This may sound strange," he continues. "But you should know how lucky you are to run into me. I can help you." The man spots my bandaged hand and stops short.

My mind starts to hum. I slashed my palm several weeks ago while scurrying up a chain-link fence. The cut is an aching inconvenience, but at least it generates sympathy when I need to solicit cash. But now I start to wonder if it's also initiated some creeping systemic infection. I've been living by myself and haven't made a careful inspection of my reflection in days. Or maybe it's even been weeks. Maybe this person sees something I can't.

"Did you not know?" the man asks. "Your hand has been very slow to heal, has it not? Didn't you find this unusual? It is a symptom of the disease. Do not be ashamed. At first my poor friend did not recognize it either. But I know how to help you."

It's true the scarlet slash across my hand hasn't properly scabbed. Maybe I have contracted a virus. Who knows what kinky microbes cling to hostel mattresses and bus station toilet seats. It's not like I feel ideal, either. I've had all kinds of health issues. But are my persistent cough and acidic stomach manifestations of something more sinister? I find myself starting to back away.

The man claps his hands to regain my attention. It's a weirdly authoritative and almost parental gesture, the way you'd deal with a distracted child. "You are sick, my friend," he says. "This is a tragic reality. Why would I lie about something like this?"

I shake my head. Not to indicate one thing or another, but to try and clear some mental space. "Do you think I am trying to take your money?" the man asks. An injured and indignant expression squirms across his face. "Look at me. Do I look like someone who needs to take advantage of anybody?"

The man is Germanic, early thirties, stylish blond crew cut, clean shaven, trim physique, blue sweater and tan slacks. "Look at my shoes," he says. "I am not joking, look at my shoes!" They're brown leather loafers with a discrete black circle, doubtless some chic designer insignia, stitched above the toes. "Tell me why someone wearing these shoes would take advantage? I do not require anyone's time or money."

He brushes his fingertips along the small of my back, subtly guiding us in the direction of a shopping thoroughfare off the main boulevard. "Call me Gert-Jan," the man says. "I would be very pleased to help you. This is my nature. I know a doctor. It is very fortunate that he is not far away." I haven't agreed to anything but there is something about his demeanor that feels reassuring.

Gert-Jan maintains a brisk commentary while we walk. There are details about his sick friend and the location of the doctor, but I'm more interested in the store fronts. The shops are closed and the lights extinguished. As we pass, I scour the glass for signs of illness in my reflection. I try to detect what Gert-Jan has noticed. Maybe others have seen it and been too polite or indifferent to react. Of course we're moving too quickly for a proper diagnosis. But I do strike myself as particularly pale and hollow-eyed.

We hurry through a small concrete courtyard and descend a flight of metal stairs to a basement office. "Here it is," Gert-Jan announces. We stand in front of a frosted glass door with the emblem of a medical cross neatly etched across the front. A comforting sight. There's a doctor's name and traces of some other information in a smaller font. Gert-Jan brandishes a silver key and lets us inside.

The office is deserted. The overpowering odor of disinfectant stings the air. The wooden floor is scarred with scratch marks. Narrow windows line the top of the walls so that only the dingiest light filters in from the street above. I would feel better if the staff was present but before I can voice my concerns, Gert-Jan hastens to explain.

"Of course it is Sunday," he says. "Naturally, everyone is at home. They have the equipment you need. This doctor is a good friend of mine. We went to medical school together, only I never finished." I find myself caught in a constant and slippery stream of information and it's all I can do to keep my balance. I've felt invisible on the streets for so long that I have no idea how to cope with this unfamiliar undertow of kindness. Gert-Jan leads us down a narrow hallway to a circular room. "Don't worry," he says. "I know exactly what to do."

Inside the operating theater, Gert-Jan unspools a fresh roll of paper for the examining table; positions the swiveling lamps so they shine brilliantly overhead; explains how he will run several quick and painless tests. He scrubs his hands, snaps on a pair of rubber gloves, and rummages for supplies. He sets about his tasks as precisely as a technician preparing a movie set for the next shot.

While I lie on the examining table, I make a mental note of my surroundings: Small cabinets on wheels, monitors with digital displays, thin steel tools soaking in jars of colored fluid. The sidewalk is visible from a rectangular window near the ceiling and several pairs of shoes march past. On the counter lies a nylon muzzle. On the back of the door hangs a poster of a golden retriever snaring a Frisbee. I flash on a terrifying thought: This is a veterinarian's office.

I don't bolt out the door. I don't scream for help. I can't explain why I continue to lie prone on the chilly exam table. Maybe part of me is still hoping Gert-Jan will cure my supposed illness. Maybe part of me doesn't care anymore. My eyes remain shut until it's over. I struggle to keep my body wholly unresponsive while Gert-Jan ties my wrists, but my left pinky keeps bucking and jerking, as if it's acquired its own nervous system.

Afterward, he removes the gag and cups my chin while I cough. "You are cured," he announces. He still wears one of the powdery green surgical gloves. It's dappled with droplets of blood.

For a long time, I lie motionless on the examining table.

Everything feels unreal, as if a critical part of myself has been unplugged. When I finally sit upright, he regards me with something approximating tenderness, maybe what you might feel for an injured pet. Gert-Jan holds out a handful of neon yellow pills and I swallow them without asking what they'll do. They tingle on my tongue and dissolve in a quick fizz.

Gert-Jan strokes my shoulder. He tousles his fingers through my hair. He leans in to kiss my lips. "You are a sad person," he says. "But I promise you will never feel any more pain."

■ ■ ■ ■ ■

Ignore the dead body on the floor. It's just earning a living. Gert Jan instructs the partygoers to step over it as they ferry rounds of drinks from the kitchen to the den. Everyone is careful not to disturb the body's composure. It lies face-down in a puddle created by the unplugged refrigerator. Its skinny arms are bound behind its back with black bandanas. The tag around its neck reads "My Name Is Jeff." The body is mine, technically speaking. But let's not get hung up on unnecessary details.

The body is in its typical corpse pose. One of them, anyway. Its white T-shirt is soaked and ideally transparent. Its mouth emits discreet bubbles in the puddled water. Its eyes are open but unmoving. They're perfectly dull, which takes more skill than you might imagine. The body isn't paying much attention to the party. I'm there but I'm not there, which is as close as I can come to describing the situation without devolving into metaphysics.

The body's eyes register a new shape swimming in front of them. A middle-aged woman with bushy chestnut curls and tiny sparrow hands. She stares intently at the body. She occasionally bends low to study its nonexistent expression. There is eye contact, of a sort. The body can't tell whether the woman wants to buy it or not. Her gaze has an unfocused intensity that would be hard to read even in the best of circumstances.

A clock chimes in the next room. Corpse time is over. Too bad. It's always been one of the body's favorite tasks. Gert-Jan unties the body and arranges it into a more traditionally enticing pose: Seated on the floor, hair ruffled over its eyes, arms tightly hugging its scuffed pink knees. "This is for your own good," Gert-Jan likes to remind the body. He hands it another yellow pill which it dutifully swallows.

The main room of the brownstone has a shimmering crimson glow. The walls have been painted silver. Red scarves are draped over the lamps to lend the place an even more exotic atmosphere. It makes the dozen people hovering over the body look like crew members on a low-budget slasher film. Grips and gaffers, maybe. Someone throws an empty wine glass into the cold black fireplace, but nobody bothers to react.

Gert-Jan announces the opening of an auction. Someone shouts out a price. Another person counters with a higher offer. The middle-aged woman remains silent, seated on the leather couch with her back to the others. Another bid. Gert-Jan announces that none of them is satisfactory. Goddamn insulting, really. He reminds everyone of the body's tender age, the distinct opportunities afforded by such barely corrupted flesh, et cetera. His accent ices the words with a superfluous layer of innuendo.

The final round of offers. While others volley a sequence of escalating digits, the body clandestinely focuses its attention in the direction of the middle-aged woman. Something sets her apart from the usual clientele. Her matronly wool sweater, stud earrings, and plaid skirt are hopelessly conservative. Her permed curls are decades out of fashion. But those aren't the real aberrations. It's how she acts so sober. Or maybe so nervous. She keeps straightening her skirt, smoothing the tight pleats with her palms then tugging primly at the hem. The body registers all this somewhere at the tingling cortex level. Call it a vague feeling of unease. If that's even close to the right emotion.

We've got a winner. An emaciated grandfather in cowboy boots jabs two fingers into the air. It's either a sardonic gesture of victory or an aggressive fuck you. At another time this detail would be a clue, but for now the body can only register the reliable drone of Gert-Jan counting out the old man's money. Gert-Jan briefly fans the bills before the body. "Business is good tonight, partner," he says, then slips the cash into his front pocket.

In a tinny voice, the body says, "Thank you." Its vocabulary has been distilled to two phrases. For its own good, really. Anything other than "Thank you" or "I'm sorry" inevitably leads to savage misunderstandings or agonizing guilt. Trust me: It's much happier this way. You'd be amazed how these four words ably express the full range of its emotions. Or rather, whatever emotional residue still remains inside the body, clinging like washed-out pigment to the walls of some long-forgotten cave.

Back to work. The old man fastens his bony fingers to the body's shoulder and guides it toward the staircase. The hazy fluorescent gleam of the open bedroom beckons at the top of the landing. The body can feel the middle-aged woman's gaze trailing its wobbly gait as it navigates the stairs. It catches a glimpse of her slowly rising to her feet. There appears to be something she wants to say, but the bedroom door slams shut and no words get spoken.

This next part's a blur. There's a plastic baggie full of pale green powder. There's a whinnying nasal voice scolding, "You weren't supposed to snort it *all*." There's the grandfather guy who's just now switching off the overhead light in the bedroom and trying in vain to kick off his cowboy boots. They're like snakes whose skins refuse to be shed. Now the light is back on. In the background, the desiccated figure of the old man has been replaced by a stocky construction worker. The body lies on the rim of a saggy black mattress and whispers, "I'm sorry." But it's in response to something someone said hours ago.

Now a chorus of voices murmurs over the body. The bedroom lights strobe off and on in slow motion. Unclassifiable sensations spread and dissolve through the body. There's a peculiar throb, reminiscent of a finger plucking the granule of hard pit from the center of a peeled grape. Behind the reddish darkness of its eyelids, warm and stinging colors bloom like fireworks against a flat night sky. Its toes curl, its back spasms and flexes, its fingers coil into tiny fists. Its jaw lowers like a drawbridge but there's no sound, no indication of either pain or pleasure.

Later the body finds itself seated on the leather couch in the living room. The party is in full swing. A hiccupping electronic beat blares over the speakers. There's a jumble of hands thumping out conversational points to the manic rhythm. A number of guests have donned festive masks. Black masks with sequins, white masks with feathers, red masks with long crooked noses. The body suspects it may be wearing a mask too. If so, that's its only item of clothing. It's stark naked except for being wrapped in a strand of red and green Christmas lights.

The middle-aged woman sits nearby, fingering one of the blinking threads of lights. Her brown curls appear more unruly. Her lips tremble and her chest heaves, as if she's trying to suppress some erupting emotion. "We need to talk," she whispers. At least the body thinks that's what she says. The woman reaches for a tall glass of what's probably vodka. The drink sloshes violently, half the contents landing with a splash on her plaid skirt. The body realizes she's no longer so sober. If she ever was.

A young blonde bursts into the brownstone. The front door swings open and she tumbles inside with a gasp. Maybe she was one of the partygoers earlier this evening. Or some other time. A column of cold air and snowflakes squalls into the room after her. Car horns and ambulance sirens blare in the distance. The blonde's pupils are glazed over with excitement. "There's been a terrible accident," she announces. "Tractor-trailer jackknife. Cars piled up everywhere. Bleeding people wandering the street."

The partygoers exchange muddled looks. Several remove their masks. At this late juncture, their ragged minds are unsure whether to treat the announcement as fresh fodder for conversation or a distant tragedy to be ignored. Even Gert-Jan seems baffled. The blonde shakes the snow off her jacket. She claps her hands together and clarifies the meaning of her message. "It's totally awesome," she says.

Gert-Jan instructs the partygoers to grab flashlights from the closet. They'll tramp out to the street to check out the smash-up. What the fuck. The party was getting predictable anyhow. Nobody bothers to give the body instructions, so it remains seated, brilliantly lit and slightly shivery. It watches the blonde lead a single-file line of unsteady souls into the night, masks resting atop their heads, clutching half-full bottles and tripping over half-laced boots.

The middle-aged woman lingers in the doorway. She's the last one left. But instead of chasing the roving flashlight beams, she shuts the door. She stands directly in front of the body. "I'm Naomi," she says loudly, as if afraid it might be hearing impaired. Her breath reeks of grain alcohol and chewed cashews. Her mouth gleams sensuously from a fresh coat of lip gloss that only partly camouflages the fuzz of a menopausal mustache. "I want to help you," she says. "But there isn't much time."

The body nods. It has no idea what she's talking about. She snatches an unfinished glass of emerald liqueur off the coffee table and polishes it off in a single surging swallow, oblivious to the liquid dribbling down her chin. Without further preamble, she yanks the plug for the Christmas lights from the wall. All the dazzling colors encircling the body go dark. As if someone has extinguished its halo. The dead strands of lights sag and flutter around its limbs as she pulls the body toward the upstairs bedroom, the limp cord and exposed plug dragging a few paces behind.

The woman shuts the door behind them. She removes the mask from the body's face, then begins to unravel the string of lights. "We better do this quickly," she says. "The others will be back soon." The body remains motionless as her woozy fingers untangle the strands, slurring together the interwoven wires on its hairless chest, slender arms, shakily bowed legs. Once she's done, the woman heaves open the bedroom window and ducks her head into the night. The curtains billow and deflate behind her. A few lost snowflakes filter into the room. No idea what she spies out there. "The monsters," she says. "The things they've made you do."

The body nods. The woman seems to be awaiting some reply, but it isn't sure how to respond to her look. After a moment, it says: "Thank you."

She turns toward the body. For the first time, her eyes seem to register how it is perfectly nude. Its smooth cock and balls have begun to shrink in the chill breeze. Its raw elbows and splayed feet quiver ever so slightly. Its otherwise unblemished skin is crisscrossed with indentations from the strands of miniature light bulbs, forming traces of a ghostly treasure map. "Don't be afraid," the woman says softly. "I'm going to help you get out of here."

The body pays no attention to her words. It's fixated on her facial expression, which has done a weird somersault now that they're sitting together on the black mattress. Some subset of emotions is imploding behind her eyes. She stutters something but the syllables are still-born. Her pinky traces the pointy vertebrae down the body's back, as if deciphering a coded message in Braille. She leans over and kisses the body on the mouth.

When their tongues touch, the woman jumps back. She exaggeratedly wipes her mouth with the hem of her wool sweater. Then she spits in the body's face. A thick gob lands between its eyebrows and slaloms down the bridge of its nose. Traces of her cherry gloss are smudged on its puffy lips. "Little pervert," she hisses. "You should be ashamed of yourself."

The body betrays no sign of emotion. The blankness of its features is so pure that it seems prepared to reflect this emptiness indefinitely. But then it does something surprising. It licks the traces of saliva from the tip of its nose and says, "I'm sorry."

The woman's mascara-framed eyes flood with dark tears. Her tiny hands cover her face so only a penumbra of frizzy brown hair remains visible. She speaks in choked and cautious tones, as if she has a baby bird cradled inside her mouth. "I'm the one who should be sorry," she whispers. "You're just a child. I have my own children who aren't much older than you." Her voice splinters into silence. She's drunk enough to be undone by her own revelation.

There are voices outside. Squeals of laughter and drifting cat-calls break through the hum of the avenue below. It's the partygoers returning from their sightseeing expedition. Someone retches the contents of their stomach onto the stoop. Gert-Jan hums the half-remembered chorus of a German football chant. The woman grips the body's shoulders. "There's not much time," she says. "Listen carefully to what I'm going to tell you."

She puts her mouth next to the body's ear and whispers a breathless litany of directions to follow, street addresses, house descriptions, people's names, pager digits. There's a heartfelt urgency to this information that confuses the body. "Remember this," the woman says. "And as soon as there's an opportunity to get away, you follow these instructions."

The body's expression remains fixed, but signs of excitement surface in its pores. A tiny tadpole-shaped muscle in its forehead begins to beat, like a second heart. The woman repeats the information: the numbers of safe houses, the names of benefactors, the paths of escape. It's impossible to tell how much the body is absorbing, but its lips move ever so slightly, as if trying to repeat the syllables.

The partygoers tramp into the old brownstone. The floor reverberates from the vibrations of slammed doors and stamping feet. The mingled voices form a distinct but undifferentiated din. Someone in the living room switches on the stereo and a dramatic burst of strings and wailing vox spills from the speakers. An aria, mid-flight. The music could be a cue. A few seconds later, Gert-Jan bursts through the bedroom door. He has a failsafe radar for trouble.

Gert-Jan's eyes flit between the open window and Naomi's conspiratorial posture. "Here is a disappointment," he says. Two partygoers grab the woman under the armpits and drag her from the room. Her shoes plow useless ruts in the carpet, unable to slow her exit. Between muffled sobs, she shouts out phone numbers and street names.

Gert-Jan locks the bedroom door. He looks at the body with a charged expression that it has as much chance of solving as a differential equation. The body instinctively cowers deeper into the mattress. Its sunken spaniel eyes blink furiously. It suddenly appears aware of its nakedness and cups both hands over its shriveled genitals. It tries to summon the words to communicate its emotions, but they surface as mere flecks of foam.

The body's teeth chatter. Gert-Jan shuts the window. He wraps the strand of Christmas lights around the body's shoulders like a shawl. The party rages on below. Bursts of drunken laughter and throbbing music. "It's okay," Gert-Jan soothes. "I know you're a good boy. I know you weren't listening to any of her nonsense."

He leans over and whispers in the body's ear. At first, the body believes he's reciting some endearment in German. But soon it realizes these are purely invented syllables. The stream of intimate gibberish begins to erase the woman's instructions, as if the idea of escape is an elaborate joke, as if every word eventually means the exact same thing. Gert-Jan presses his lips closer. The whispering continues. It's as if I'm not even here.

■ ■ ■ ■ ■

I'm dreaming upside down. I mean, I'm upside down and dreaming. My feet are propped at the head of the bed and the sheets twist in whorls around my ankles. My naked body twitches ever so slightly. Are my eyelids fluttering? It looks like. If you could crawl behind them, you would find yourself in the middle of a grassy field at night. The moon shines brightly overhead. A lone orange tree stands in the distance. A warm breeze tickles the undersides of its leaves so that orbs of fruit can be seen glistening on its branches. They're ripe for the taking. And where am I in this dream? Lying in the grass and contemplating distant constellations. Content to be a bystander, even in my own imagination.

My eyelids definitely flutter this time. Some bubble of consciousness ripples its way to the surface. I roll over and groan. Reptile-brain tells me to yawn. I stretch the hinges of my jaw. Reptile-brain tells me to open my eyes. I make little slits of them. From the bruise-colored light filtering through the window, it must be some early hour of the morning. The shadows in the bedroom slowly coalesce into familiar shapes. The cramped apartment is eerily silent.

Reptile-brain tells me to finger my crotch. It's a little crusty. I start to feel guilty about something from last night. Not totally sure what it is yet. Still I feel bad about it. Reptile-brain tells me to sit up. Immediately the back of my neck begins to tingle. There's somebody else in the bed. An indistinct figure is heaped under the patchwork quilt adorned with sailboats. A small foot sticks out from under the frayed fabric.

I can't recall anything about its owner. The foot's chipped toenails are painted green, probably some sort of clue. Reptile-brain tells me to look closer. I take another peek at the body. It's asleep, probably. Completely still, certainly. There's another option, but I refuse to consider it. I don't want to know. There's probably a good reason for not wanting to know, but I don't want to know that either.

Instead, I stare at the half-drunk glass of soda. The fluid is flat, all the bubbles gone, wherever bubbles go when they're no more. An old cigarette butt lies curled at the bottom of the glass, immersed in the dead amber liquid. It looks larval. The ashy black tip resembles a tail dropping spores. This glass of soda is suddenly and truly the most fascinating object I have ever seen. Or to put it another way: It's the one object in this room that I can deal with, the only one seemingly free of unsettling associations. I stare at the glass for a full five minutes.

Slowly my vision expands to include a bottle of neon yellow pills. It sits next to the glass. The twist-top is slightly askew. Gert-Jan must be passed out in the living room because otherwise he would have knocked on the door by now. He doesn't allow the partygoers to sleep in the bedroom with me. "It's dangerous to let them get too close," he says. "I found out the hard way when I was your age."

My usual routine would be to shake the foot and point to the door. But Reptile-brain suggests that I should be the one to leave instead. I stand up and pull a pair of jeans and my green sweater from a heap on the floor. Quickly paste them onto my body. Add a pair of muddy tennis shoes to my feet. Lick my palm and arrange my stringy black hair in the mirror. Careful not to look too closely at anything else.

Too late. Something catches my eye: It's my dream, reflected back to me in the mirror. I mean, it's a reproduction of the painting I ripped from one of Gert-Jan's magazines. The image of the lone orange tree is stuck to the wall above the bed with thumbtacks. A picture of terrible totemic power. You can get seriously lost in it. Reptile-brain tells me to leave it and not chance waking up the body. That is, if the body can even be awakened. Reptile-brain assures me it isn't worth the risk. But I rip the image off the wall anyway and stuff it in my back pocket.

I tiptoe down the narrow hallway. Reptile-brain instructs me to be especially quiet. Soft snores issue from the darkened living room. A handful of revelers lie slumped across the ravaged couches. As I thread my way through the room, a man with a massive bushy beard stirs and squints at me. He begins to beckon with an outstretched hand but drifts back into unconsciousness before he can complete the gesture.

Gert-Jan is positioned by the front door, curled in a shapeless armchair. An occasional smile creeps across his sleeping lips. He's forbidden me to leave the apartment complex, but Reptile-brain insists on getting more distance from this place. I push open the door and stumble outside. A thick night fog shrouds the building's concrete breezeway. Reptile-brain tells me to make for the stairs. I take the steps two at a time, but it almost feels like I haven't left. It's as if the gloomy weather is just an extension of the apartment.

I reach the sidewalk but have no idea which way to turn. Reptile-brain says any direction is the right direction. I start walking alongside a desolate strip of freeway, listening for the rumble of distant traffic. I can't remember the last time I was outside. The mist shrouds the rows of rusting factories and rotting warehouses that hang back from the highway. The overhead constellations are little more than rumors. Further down the road, I make out the smeared neon lights of a bodega. Reptile-brain suggests some food.

The store inhabits the shell of an abandoned garage. Smudges of motor oil fresco the far corners of the walls. There are no other customers in the place. Under buzzing fluorescent lights, I roam the two skinny aisles. I pass packets of laundry soap, party balloons, multi-colored shoelaces. I finger bags of chocolate marshmallows, dried noodles, jellied fruit. Suddenly I know what I need in the way of nourishment: smokes.

The cigarettes will be at the cash register. Wherever that is. I scan the aisles and spot the checkout tucked away at the rear of the store. A brown-skinned man behind the counter glares at me. I realize I probably don't have any cash and plunge an exploratory hand into the front pocket of my jeans. I come up with a massive wad of bills. Far more money than I expected. My heart leaps into my lungs, making it hard to breathe. Reptile-brain instructs me to peel off one bill and shove the rest back in my pocket. Fair enough.

I slap the bill on the counter and gesture at a pack of cigarettes emblazoned with a snarling pit bull. The clerk taps the hand-lettered sign affixed to the side of the cash register. It says the store doesn't accept large bills. For the first time, I notice the stratospheric denomination of my currency. I've never even seen the figurehead engraved on the front. The clerk shakes his head and shoves the bill back at me.

Reptile-brain tells me to leave, but I want those cigarettes. I lean across the counter and grab one of the packs. The clerk becomes apoplectic, punching the counter and pointing to the door. He shouts a stream of angry syllables. It's probably just as well the dialogue comes across as pure sound. I mean, words would be too heavy for me at this point.

I pocket the smokes and dash out of the store. Reptile-brain tells me not to look back. I run recklessly through the fog. The only thing I can make out are the fresh squares of concrete that keep appearing in front of my feet. The sidewalk seems to be moving like a conveyor belt. Every so often, the milk-blue glow of a streetlamp passes overhead. I try to tally them to determine how far I've traveled, but I soon lose track. Reptile-brain suggests a place up ahead to cross the freeway.

I sprint headlong across the four lanes. Once I reach the other side, I turn in the opposite direction, determined to leave a cold trail for any pursuers. My head feels pumped full of helium. It's as if I'm high or maybe hung-over or maybe even experiencing some variation on normal. I walk deeper into the whiteness. The high-beams of passing trucks occasionally tunnel through the fog. In the distance, a five-story building slowly takes shape.

I find myself crossing two lanes of traffic and heading toward this structure. It's a beacon in the bleached terrain. As the night drains away, I stand on a grassy strip of median and inspect its brick architecture and darkened façade. A solitary window on the third floor is lit up. A silhouette flits in and out of the frame. It takes a moment to realize I'm back where I started. The fit-fully pacing figure is Gert-Jan.

Reptile-brain insists that I flee the scene, but my feet remain moored on the median. I'm hypnotized by the painted lines of the highway. The pattern of dotted and unbroken lines, the yellow and white stripes, form a sort of code. The message is easily cracked: All pathways lead to the same point.

I sit down on the traffic island. This overgrown patch of grass seems as good a place as any to figure things out. The occasional delivery truck rattles past and I imbibe the rippling plumes of diesel exhaust. A glass bottle lies tangled in the weeds. Several yellowish swallows of dirty vodka remain in the bottom. They leave a sweet and burning aftertaste.

I try to form some thoughts about the money. Reptile-brain doesn't know where it came from, so I'm on my own. I stretch one of the bills between my fingers and examine the portrait of an unfamiliar man in a powdered wig. A microscopic amount of crosshatches form the details of the arched eyebrows, the haughty cast of the eyes, the fractionally upturned mouth that seems to prophesy a smirk. I'm pretty certain the money isn't the answer either. It's probably a trap set by Gert-Jan. Something planted in my pockets as a test.

An idea: I take my lighter and place the flame against the edge of the bill. Several moments pass, then the cash ignites and crumples into a tail of ash. The black smoke gives off a faintly sweet whiff, a mixture of wet hay and something sugary. Cinnamon, maybe. The tiny bonfire is a gorgeous conflagration of blue flames that vanishes as quickly as a mirage. I can't say why, but I know this is the right thing to do.

I light another bill. More smoke, et cetera. Maybe it's just the combination of the vodka, the ambient hum of the roadway, and the smell of burning money, but things are starting to make sense in a way they haven't before. I light the rest of the bills. The figure in the building across the street leans out of the third-story window. He shouts something. The sense is lost in the squall of a speeding taxi.

Another idea: I carefully unfold the image of the painting from my back pocket. It fits perfectly in the palm of my hand. Looking at this picture is like being back in my dream. I sit there and watch myself watching the orange tree. This is somehow important. It's my dream but it isn't. It's like I'm dreaming the image. Or maybe it's dreaming me. There is a momentary distraction as an 18-wheel truck honks its horn. I spot Gert-Jan standing on the sidewalk across the highway. He calls out my name.

Reptile-brain pleads with me to run. To simply stand up and start moving my legs. I tune it out. This is more important. The painting of the orange tree holds an answer and it isn't going to elude me. As I stare deeper into the image, there is an odd sensation that I'm already in another dream. A real-life dream, say. It signifies something important, though I'm not sure what.

Soon I'm not alone on the traffic island. Gert-Jan's shadow drapes itself over my scrawny frame. He curses under his breath and removes his belt. But I'm not worried. For the first time in months, I can almost start to imagine what it might feel like to be awake.

I must be hatching plans behind my back. It's the only explanation for why I'm so calm. I lounge on the sofa in the new apartment and watch indifferently as Gert-Jan signs for another round of deliveries. We moved here after he decided we needed "a change of the scene." Gert-Jan rented this sprawling loft and set about masterminding some renovations. The floor is littered with a mystifying mishmash of materials. Stacks of lumber, metal pipes, acetylene torches. Rolls of black velvet, pulleys, ropes. Gert-Jan provides emphatic instructions to the workmen about how some soundproofing material should be installed. "My hearing is so sensitive," he tells one of them. I listen to this lie with unusual poise. Not even my pinky trembles.

My eyes scan the swarm of activity, but my expression remains neutral. It's difficult to say what I might be up to. These days I'm on a need-to-know basis with myself. My gaze circles back to the spiral staircase in the corner of the room. Most of the materials are being loaded down its corkscrew steps. I have no idea what's in the basement. I listen for clues but even the clanging footsteps of the workers are swallowed by the darkness.

When the last workman has vanished downstairs, Gert-Jan approaches wearing a philosophical smile. "This is a time of changes," he says. "That body you left in the last place created a hassle, but it gave me exciting ideas." He tousles my shaggy black locks. "You cause the problems and I make the even better solutions. We are not a bad team."

He hands me a bright yellow pill. I palm it through an elegant slight of hand and pantomime a swallow. No idea where that move came from. I surreptitiously slip the capsule inside the front pocket of my jeans. It's the first time I haven't taken my daily dosage. This must have something to do with my plan.

The rest of the afternoon I pretend to be strung out, but clearly I'm searching for something. There's an unmistakable intensity to my examination of the white plaster walls, the curved arc of the ceiling, the chandelier with its dangling rows of glass baubles. I also notice myself keeping close track of Gert-Jan's movements. He spends hours on the phone, talking in clipped and coded phrases, arranging more deliveries for the next morning. He fills his day planner with pager digits, account numbers, and a rough sketch of an unknown contraption. It's hard to tell if this bothers me. I watch myself for clues, but I'm not giving anything away.

At night I can't sleep. My body feels peculiar without chemicals circulating through its system. I'm still wide awake when Gert-Jan begins to thrash around in the covers. His chest is wracked with panting heaves, as if he's struggling against a current. His face is slick with sweat. He urgently mumbles a few words in German. Then he sits upright in bed and screams.

I remain perfectly motionless, not daring to reveal that I've witnessed this. Soon he lies down and falls fast asleep. I'm afraid to speculate about what could give him nightmares. I tell myself that it's not a sinister omen or haunting pang of bad conscience. It's merely a random circuit tripped and reset. But these thoughts fail to slow the escalating thrum of my heartbeat.

In the morning, I find myself reluctant to pry open my eyes. I try to ignore the droning chime of the doorbell, the muffled deliberations of delivery men, the ripping open of sealed cardboard boxes. Gert-Jan balances on the bed frame and hands me a yellow pill. Once again, I palm it and fake the swallow. Another deposit for my collection. "Welcome to a big day," Gert-Jan tells me.

The living area is a hive of workmen. There's an array of rarified materials, including a round mirror in an ornate wooden frame. Plus plenty of shiny metal tools that I can't name. One of the contractors approaches me with a tape measure and tells me to spread out my arms. He avoids looking at me while collecting my measurements. Later, I overhear him discussing me with a coworker. He uses the word "prototype."

One by one, the boxes disappear into the basement. Gert-Jan inscribes a firm mark in his notebook to indicate the descent of each item. He's completely absorbed by this slow procession. The lines of his brow are bunched in a peculiar way, as if the tense geometry of his face is mimicking the plans that he's busy drafting. I don't look too closely. "You will stay up here," he tells me.

I sit myself in the window alcove. It overlooks the street a few stories below. A bland view of an empty cul-de-sac. Concrete apartment buildings with oily curtains drawn. Overflowing metal trash cans bunched on the curb. I act oblivious to the reverberations of the workmen marching up and down the circular stairs, their shoes clanking against the metal steps in a relentless springy rhythm. I take a pack of gum from my jeans and unwrap a single foil stick. I chew without registering the flavor.

Eventually the noises of the workmen subside. From the back pocket of my jeans, I remove the image of the orange tree in the empty field. It's so worn that the colors are starting to rub away. I stare into this talisman for several moments. There I am, lost somewhere in its fathomless depths. Then I carefully refold the picture and hop down from the alcove. I don't betray the slightest hint of emotion, even to myself.

Now the plan gets underway. There I am, frantically searching the contents of the remaining cardboard boxes and rustling through the leftover packing materials. My hands seem to be scavenging for something in particular. All the while, I listen for the clanging sound of feet on the circular metal steps. I have no idea what I'm preparing to do until I climb onto a chair and fling a strand of twine over the top of the chandelier.

I thread the rope through the chain that attaches the chandelier to the ceiling. I'm not sure how my fingers know how to braid the contortions of that particular knot. Then I loop the twine into a noose and squeeze it over my head. It feels uncomfortably sturdy. There must be some way to stop this, but then my feet knock over the chair.

My body plummets. My stomach rebounds into my throat with a sharp kick. There's a searing burn from the unfraying rope. My pulverized Adam's apple. My bulging eyeballs. My gurgling last unformed syllables. My body pitching and kicking over open space.

The chandelier chain starts to tremble. The tart jingle of glass overhead is followed by a loud ripping sound, as if the ceiling is a sheet of paper being torn in half. I feel myself falling again. My knees and elbows clatter against the wooden floor. The chandelier crashes on top of me and spikes my forehead into the ground. My skull is a dull throb. My entire body feels like it's ringing.

There I am, trying to fight free of the wreckage. I wrestle through the tangled strands of wire and nuggets of broken glass. I lurch a few steps forward and begin to gag. The noose is still fastened around my neck and I'm dragging the shattered chandelier behind me. I stagger another few steps. I'm heading straight for the window, probably planning to finish the job with a headfirst dive.

I'm pretty sure I hear footsteps trampling up the staircase behind me. I focus my sights on the window, stiffen my neck, and propel myself a few feet ahead. Every successive step hurts more. My forehead pounds. There's blood in my mouth. The scraping sound of the trailing chandelier fills the entire room. The frame of the window is almost within reach, but the light keeps growing fainter. A sudden eclipse, maybe. I muster the energy for one last lunge. The light is almost totally extinguished now. The eclipse is at full... or whatever...

When I regain consciousness, I find myself laid out on the couch. My body aches. My forehead is bandaged with white gauze. My cheeks and arms are pocked with rivets of gashed flesh. Everything in the apartment is quiet. There's no sign of the workmen. The mess from the chandelier has been cleared away except for a few stray shards on the floor which sparkle in the periphery of my vision, like the lingering afterimage of a fireworks display.

Gert-Jan makes his entrance. I shut my eyes in anticipation of the screaming fit. He remains silent and methodically disinfects my cuts with peroxide. He hands me a glass of water. I try to swallow but my throat feels like it's been sawed in half. I start to cough. My chest strains, splutters, spumes. He urges me to take another sip and this one goes down. Gert-Jan stares at my impassive expression with almost scientific fascination, as if he's discovered a strain of cells that split in unexpected ways. "I see you in there," he says in a gentle voice. "This must be taking a toll. You are starting to look so old."

He leaves the room and returns with a glass jar of ointment and a coiled strand of rope. "This is not a worry," he says. "I've got to make us some dinner. We need to keep you from getting in trouble again." He wraps the rope snugly around the slender trunk of my body and knots it in several places. He unscrews the lid of the jar and smears my cuts with the sticky and runny salve. He lathers on a thorough coating of the stuff. It smells pretty strong, like fresh paint and spoiled yeast.

I watch him disappear into the kitchen. For the first time in ages, my mind is quiet. No furtive plans seem to be formulating. I'm able to look at the iron railings of the spiral staircase without a sense of dread. I can even ignore the chipped bits of plaster that silt like snowflakes from the fresh hole in the ceiling. I allow myself to sink into the reassuring bonds of the rope. I inhale the pleasantly stinging odor of the salve. To tell the truth, I'm almost happy.

As we get ready for bed, I notice Gert-Jan's new ritual. Before he puts on his pajamas, he holds each item to the light and runs his fingers along the seams. It's almost as if he's grown distrustful of them, combing the threads for contaminants and foreign bodies. He's not asleep long before his eyes begin to strobe beneath their lids. He winds himself in the sheets and moans agitated German phrases. He wakes himself with a guttural and terror-stricken bark. His face is turned to the wall, but he seems to be sobbing, softly.

This time, I find myself reaching over to comfort him. I place my hand against the small of his back. He doesn't shake it off. Cautiously, I wrap my arms around him. His skin is clammy and coated in chilled droplets of sweat. His face is ghostly pale. In this half-awake state, he barely seems to recognize me. I tell him everything is okay. I reassure him it was only a dream.

I climb out of bed to get him a cup of tea. I slip on my jeans and walk purposefully into the kitchen to put on the kettle. I spoon tea grounds into the mug, then add the hot water. While it steeps, my hand dives into my pocket and produces the unswallowed yellow pills. There I am, grinding them up on the counter and using the flat of my palm to scrape the powder into the mug.

I present Gert-Jan with the steaming mug of tea. I'm not sure of the exact effects of the chemicals, but they ought to knock him out for several hours. He claps the mug between his hands as if it's an alien object. There I am, waiting for him to take a sip. A moment that seems to stretch the entire length of our relationship. Finally he takes a tentative swallow. Apparently there's no aftertaste to set off alarms because he wipes his mouth and finishes the rest of it.

He yawns several times and it seems he could simply be sleepy. Then he drops the mug to the floor. Everything shatters except for the thick handle. Gert-Jan doesn't flinch from the resounding rattle. His lips spasm into a lopsided half-smile. The whites of his eyes loll lazily in their sockets. In one elegant motion, his body slides off the bed and crumples onto the floor. I'm barely aware of what comes next.

There I am, testing his unconscious body with the tip of my sneaker. I hurriedly tug on my green sweater and stuff a few remaining outfits into a bag. I stride through the living area and squeeze my eyes shut to avoid any sight of the gaping cavity in the ceiling. But even as I leave the apartment, I know I'm being pursued by that flaking rim of loose plaster, the exposed black wires, the sleeping current.

■ ■ ■ ■ ■

The posters spring up throughout the city. This afternoon I spot another one. A light blue sheet of paper stapled to a telephone pole. It features the photo of a beseeching boy and the hand-written headline "Have you seen me?" I rip down the notice without breaking stride. The two fliers up the block get the same treatment. By now it's a reflex. I nonchalantly ball the photocopies in my fist and dump them in the nearest trash can. Please ignore the fact that my hands are trembling.

These are the first posters I've seen in this part of town. They started surfacing a week ago along the dead-end avenues of the waterfront. They invaded every vacant space near the docks: Utility poles, phone kiosks, construction fences. They flushed me out of hiding. Some posters say I'm a runaway. Others claim I've been kidnapped. A few warn that I've committed a violent crime. At the bottom of each one sits details about a reward and Gert-Jan's name.

More blue posters up ahead. They hang on a succession of mailboxes and flap noisily in the breeze. I pause to examine the photo on the latest flier: I look fetching and ideally uncompli-cated. A lock of black hair flops over one eye. My lips curl into an easy smile. But if you squint closer, you can excavate the crippled expression smuggled within my gaze. It's kind of dev-astating. A fresh sea of blue pages flutter on the horizon, so I flee in the opposite direction.

I head back toward the abandoned fast food restaurant. A bankrupt burger franchise, probably. I've been staking out the place for days. A faded eviction notice is taped to the door and a padlock wrapped around the handle, but something's happening inside. Sections of the butcher paper obscuring the windows have peeled away. Through the dusty peepholes, you can spy the ripped-out kitchen fixtures, the plastic counter, the menu board dangling from the ceiling. Look closely and you'll notice the interior landscape is in constant flux. Like a time-lapse film, items materialize then vanish. Greasy food wrappers, tubes of toothpaste, sticks of deodorant. Signs of a secret life.

I squat next to the entrance. Dozens of feet walk past every few seconds. Spillover activity from the nearby bus station. This is a neighborhood of strip clubs, nail salons, all-night bars, and massage parlors. I notice a deliveryman in brown overalls ferrying a box of creams and lubricants into the peep show next door. Curiously, he walks out with the same package. I trail him down a deserted side street lined with dumpsters. He stops in front of a row of doors, presses a buzzer, then slips inside. These must be the service entrances for the businesses on the main avenue. One broken plaque stammers out the letters B-U-R-G.

I curl myself into the alcove of the service entrance and wait to see if anyone will arrive. It's nighttime before a woman with a grocery bag totters purposefully in my direction. She hobbles as if she's sprained an ankle. It takes a few seconds to realize that she's hugely pregnant. The woman distractedly digs through her purse for the keys. She doesn't notice me sitting at her feet. Instead of attempting to explain myself, I have a simpler plan: I scream.

The woman clobbers me over the head with the groceries. She frantically unlocks the door, then claps a hand over my mouth and tugs me into a concrete hallway. After securing the door, she stares at me wide-eyed. Her lips contort as if forming words, but the only sound that escapes is a violent wheeze.

The grocery bag tumbles to her feet. Her features clench in a contorted grimace. She slides onto the floor and clutches her stomach. This must be a contraction.

The woman huffs and pants. Her face gleams with sweat. When the pain subsides, I help lift her to her feet. She waddles down the service corridor without a word. I scoop up her bag and follow a few paces behind. She turns into a cave-like space that must have once been the freezer. It's been transformed into a bedroom, complete with a ratty mattress, flannel quilt, and stepstool that doubles as a bedside table. The woman lights some candles to chase away the shadows.

She collapses onto the mattress. Her hands rest flat atop her enormous belly, monitoring the frequency of the amniotic vibrations. I perch on the only other item of furniture in the room, an oversized red trunk. The woman introduces herself as Ruth. A black bandana highlights her tufts of tangled blond curls. The flowing gypsy dress accentuates her stomach and the tattoo of an insecticide can on her shoulder. I can feel her eyes examining me.

Ruth unpacks the groceries: A vial of prenatal pills, a package of beef jerky, a sleeve of crackers, and a jar of peanut butter. She scoops a fingerfull of peanut butter into her mouth. "I'd kill someone for a steak dinner," she says. She unlaces her black combat boots, peels off a pair of sooty socks, and stares at her bloated red ankles. "Have you been on the streets long?" she asks. "I can't believe I'm still doing this."

I find myself staring at Ruth's pregnant stomach. I can't help myself. "You want to touch my belly?" she says. "It's okay. It's not like a big deal." The thought makes my heart sweat, but I shake my head. There's a long silence. One of the candles sputters out. "You can stay the night," Ruth says finally. "Just keep out of sight."

After she falls asleep, I blow out the cratered candles and explore the restaurant. The place reeks of mildew and burnt plastic. The bathrooms have been stripped of ceramic tiles, but the sinks and toilets remain. The dining area is marked with the ghostly footprints of ripped-out appliances and the exposed steel of load-bearing walls. I crawl beneath the service counter and arrange my body on the chalky floor. Noises emanate from the surrounding structure, softly rattling the loose ceiling tiles. I think of Ruth and imagine the sounds are her child's heartbeat resounding within the cinderblock walls. The reverberations lull me to sleep.

Shortly after sunrise, a series of fliers slide under the front door, all of them emblazoned with my face.

I spend the day trying to distract myself. It's pointless to fixate on images of Gert-Jan prowling outside the service entrance, trading cigarette cartons for stray ends of information. Instead I help Ruth clean. She seems to enjoy the company as she kneels on the floor next to a plastic bucket and pile of wet rags, scouring every inch of her bedroom. "Too bad you didn't know me before," she says. "When I was thin. I was really something." She's a peculiar sight with the tattoo and violet sweatpants, hugely pregnant and scrubbing the cement. But there's also something unmistakably sexy about her oval belly and plump ass.

She stares at the pools of water islanded across the floor. "Maybe it's some biological nesting bullshit," she says. "But I swear it's a miracle I haven't choked on all this filth." She reaches for the bottle of Murphy Oil Soap, but it's empty. She slops the rags in the bucket in a vain effort to soak up some remaining suds. Ruth struggles to her feet and retrieves a pair of tennis shoes from the corner. "Time for more supplies," she says with an awkward grin.

After she leaves, I creep into the ruins of the dining room. I arrange myself beneath an automotive calendar that's two years old and still several months off. I'm only a few feet from the front windows. Through the scrim of butcher paper, I observe the silhouettes of pedestrians rustling past in twos and threes. The hum of chatter, hiccups of traffic, and surges of music mix together into a tidal soundscape. At some point, I must doze off.

When I open my eyes, the street lights and neon signs have flickered to life. The nighttime noises have escalated to a frothy din. At first, I don't notice the rattling sounds behind me. Then I hear Gert-Jan's voice echo through the rear corridor. His pidgin accent is unmistakable. Ruth fusses with the lock and announces in a loud voice: "There's nobody else here."

A burst of adrenalized terror rockets through my body. I dash for the bedroom and squeeze inside the oversized red trunk. It's a tight fit, but I've been practicing. Several moments later, Ruth enters and eases herself onto the mattress. She ignites several wicks. It's easy to imagine Gert-Jan positioned in the doorway, his legs casually crossed, surveying the surroundings for clues he can play to his advantage. I expect him to launch a charm offensive, but instead he speaks with halting uncertainty.

Gert-Jan says: "I much appreciate you talking with me. The boy on the fliers is an important friend of mine. I am distressed and following every information I come across. We had some terrible misunderstandings. They were my fault. I just want to apologize."

Against my will, I detect a note of genuine loss in his speech. It stimulates a flooding sensation of guilt and regret. Then it occurs to me that Gert-Jan's words aren't solely aimed at Ruth, and I squeeze myself into a tighter ball in the darkness.

Ruth finally replies. She says she doesn't know who he's talking about.

Gert-Jan says: "In fact, I am the boy's guardian. So there is a legal obligation here. It may be true some unfortunate decisions were made. But the boy is in grave danger. Surely this is the most important consideration."

Ruth repeats she doesn't know who he's talking about, but

her denial carries less conviction. I picture Gert-Jan circling the room, marking the circumference as if he owns it, as if Ruth is the one imposing herself in this scene.

Gert-Jan says: "This is the absolute truth. And it is a little sticky. I am the boy's father. Only recently I came into his life. I have tried to do my best, but the boy holds a grudge for the years I was missing." I can detect the gears in his story grinding ever so slightly. His English improves whenever his temper flares. "Unfortunately the boy suffers from a terminal illness and refuses to accept the seriousness of his situation. I can only pray he is not dead already. It would be a terrible burden for his caretaker."

Ruth says she wishes she could help, but she still doesn't know who he's talking about. Her tone is more uncertain yet. I wonder how much longer she can hold out.

Inside the trunk, my body has begun to atrophy. The story about my illness is a hoax, but I'm starting to feel its effects. My limbs clench. My head balloons. Orange-yellow spots burst across my eyelids. Or maybe I'm just running low on oxygen.

Gert-Jan says: "Let me cut right to it. I'm offering to buy the boy. For a sizable sum." There's a pause where he probably fans out a number of bills. Part of me wishes I could see exactly how much. "The boy is my property. It's only right you should turn him over."

The atmosphere thick with unspoken negotiations. I wait for the lid of the trunk to rise and those tender hands to encircle my windpipe once again.

"That's a serious offer," Ruth says. "But the kid isn't here."

Gert-Jan whistles a few high notes. His imitation of the spotted thrush. An attempt to recalibrate the tension in the room. He says: "So tell me, when is your baby due?"

"Could be any day now."

Gert-Jan says: "You must be full of plans. I envy you having a child to bring into your home."

Ruth bristles at the inflection of that last word. "This is a temporary situation."

Gert-Jan says: "Of course, of course. But the main thing is the arrival of a new life. A new beginning. This is always something to celebrate." A rustling sound. I can't picture what's transpiring. "Please accept this as a small token for imposing on you."

"That's nice and all, but I can't drink."

It's probably a bottle of wine and no doubt a formidable vintage.

Gert-Jan says: "How silly of me. Instead let me treat you to a meal. A friend of mine owns a restaurant down the street. He cooks a great steak."

An inscrutable silence follows.

He says: "Surely there is no harm in some good food. We are assured of good service. I will not take up but a little of your time."

She finally assents with a few guttural murmurs. As the two sets of footsteps echo down the service corridor, my spirits plummet. Gert-Jan's persuasions are more effective the longer he holds your attention. When I emerge from the stifling darkness of the trunk, I lie on the mattress and suck on the edges of the quilt, pulling at the loose threads with my teeth. I try not to imagine the deal he will have extracted from her before the appetizers are served.

Ruth returns sometime past dawn. She stumbles in alone and passes out on the mattress without a word. I stay awake all night. I pace the service hallway for hours hoping she'll stir. Finally I sit myself in the entrance to her bedroom. I stare at her sleeping form and listen to her nasal wheezes. There's something soothing about the rhythmic fluctuations of her stomach.

It happens in slow motion. I find myself creeping toward her. Each step is completely silent. Soon my hand hovers a few inches above her belly. I slowly lower my palm. Her belly feels unreal, like the rind of a ripe melon. Everything is placid, then

I feel a tiny-but-definite kick. It's as if the baby knows I'm here. It's reaching out to greet me.

When Ruth wakes several hours later, no mention is made of Gert-Jan. She shuffles around her room, compulsively shifting, straightening, and reshifting every item. Her eyes meet mine and she smiles. The sort of convoluted and heartbroken expression that conceals entire histories. It feels like she's about to confess something, but the moment passes. "You know, for a moment I could swear I saw what you looked like as a child," she says. "It must have been pretty sad." I can't help blushing, not because of the words but the attention.

Ruth announces she's going shopping. She hauls herself down the service corridor and pauses with her hand on the lock. "Some friends are throwing a party tonight," she says. "You should come." She turns the handle and vanishes onto the side-walk. And just like that, the hinge of fate swings into place. This party must be where Gert-Jan has arranged to get me back.

Half in a daze, I wander into the dining room. I stare at the divots in the floor where the booths had been bolted. I stick my fingers in the gouges, wondering how difficult it was to dislodge these pieces and if the furniture put up much of a fight.

I'm not the only one watching Ruth dance. People marvel at the sight of a pregnant woman in this crowded loft, shifting her swollen belly to the morphing rhythms. Sweat christens her brow. Her cheeks flush crimson. The white crescents of her eyes shine between her lids. She looks exquisite. Each movement radiates a sense of pure abandon. Ruth is the only reason I agreed to attend the party. The night will probably end badly and watching her dance may be my sole consolation. But right now, it's enough.

The loft spans the third floor of an old textile warehouse. A mirrored ball rotates from the ceiling, dappling the cavernous space with squares of light. It highlights the various factions on the dance floor. The kinetic exhibitionists whose bodies whip and reel in intricate spasms. The autistic introverts who rock rhythmically on their heels while staring blankly at the speakers. And Gert-Jan. My blood freezes and my irises turn pale, but the man with the blond crew cut rotates to reveal a different face.

As the song hiccups to a halt, Ruth shakes off her trance and squints into the darkness. I stand against the wall of industrial windows and flash an ungainly smile to indicate my presence. Ruth wobbles in my direction. She shakes the sticky curls loose from her forehead and takes the beer from my hand. She chugs the contents, then inspects the bottles lining the ledge. She finds one that's almost full and knocks that back as well. She offers a defiant shrug. "What the hell," she says. "You only die once."

A concussive bass line shakes the wooden floor and Ruth shivers in recognition. She wades into the mass of dancers, unsteady on her feet but unwilling to miss another note. I need some air and stick my head out one of the cantilevered windows. Across the street, I notice another warehouse party is in full swing. Its smeared red lights pulse like a beacon from another world. I need to clear my head, but the music continues to pummel at escalating frequencies. It steadily builds toward an unknown climax.

There's a commotion on the dance floor. Ruth is prostrate on the ground, writhing in pain. She must have launched herself into labor. Several men hoist her body above the crowd. She lies on her back like an Egyptian queen, her distended belly facing the ceiling as they ferry her toward the bathroom. Somebody briefly loses their grip and there's the strange sight of Ruth's disembodied feet kicking the air. The music continues to blare from trembling speakers. One of the men straining to keep Ruth aloft—this time I'm positive—is Gert-Jan.

Things begin to jumble. A dozen people encircle the wet spot on the dance floor where her water must have broken. A man in a tuxedo ambles into the crowd with upraised palms to assure everyone the situation is under control. Then the sirens start to wail. They originate from the street though I can't figure how ambulances could have arrived so quickly. The DJ spins a sultry ballad to mellow the crowd, but the effect is undercut by paramedics plunging into the loft carrying a canvas stretcher. A small throng rings the bathroom. They block the entrance to the stalls. They strain on tiptoes to steal a view of the action. Somebody shouts the baby is starting to crown.

Gert-Jan must be inside the bathroom but there are too many bodies colliding from too many directions to tell. Nobody can even hear the paramedics, who shove their way into the stalls with enthusiastic brutality. I'm surprised Gert-Jan hasn't come after me, but I'm not lingering to complain. As I stumble for the exit, the music vibrates in my teeth. The taste of vomit tickles my throat. I navigate the archipelago of people huddled in conversation and twitching in time to the slow-burn soul. A couple squirms on the drink table, knocking over bottles as they make out. Somehow I manage not to glance back at the bathroom.

When I reach the stairwell, the narrow steps sway under my feet, so I shut my eyes and blindly grope my way down toward the street. Behind me, the DJ cues a new song.

It rains constantly the next few days. I stay out of sight while maintaining a stealthy vigil near the abandoned fast food restaurant. It's hard to understand why Gert-Jan didn't grab me at the party, but I'm not taking any chances. I camp in the alley across from the service entrance, folding myself into the shadows and huddling among the overflowing trash bags. The restaurant is uncannily quiet. The only evidence of life is a pair of contractors who tape a building permit across the front door.

I'm attuned to the slightest indication of pursuit, but so far there's no ripple of activity. Gert-Jan is usually more efficient.

Behind the bus station, I spot a raft of familiar blue fliers that have been battered by the weather. They're bleached and near wordless. Lonely black smudges left behind to keep lookout. A teenage girl staples handmade posters about a lost dog over them. Only one flier remains visible on the wall, but I don't tear it down.

Each day I spend a few hours panhandling for change. I mark up cardboard signs with random chapters and verses from the Bible. John 45:12. Matthew 6:55. Luke 36:3. People assume they reference some profound message of charity, so I do pretty well. I even manage a few extra items with the money. I buy a plastic baby doll for Ruth's new infant. Plus I pick up a five-inch switchblade for protection.

I'm consolidating my change one afternoon when I spot him. Gert-Jan cuts a decisive path through the waves of weary tourists and commuters. We share a frozen moment of eye contact. Instinctively, I crumple into myself like a hermit crab. My body tenses for the worst, but Gert-Jan brushes past as if I'm another face in the hustling crowd. When he pauses at the corner, I see he has something in his arms. The traffic light changes and he hurries into the grid of the crosswalk. As he strides in front of the idling barricade of taxis, it's obvious. Gert-Jan is holding a baby. Its tiny bald head pokes from a blue wool blanket. The infant doesn't look more than a few days old.

For several stunned moments, my body remains paralyzed. Then I find myself bolting across the avenue in pursuit. A sea of undifferentiated figures stretches in front of me, but Gert-Jan and the baby can't be more than a block ahead. I dodge the horns of oncoming autos and crane my neck for a better view. The crowd briefly thins to reveal a guiding glimpse of Gert-Jan's crew cut. I bound past concrete planters filled with mums, swerve around trash cans and light poles, push aside businesswomen on their cell phones. Then abruptly I lose sight of them.

They must have entered the bus station. I fight my way

through the surging crowds and scurry past the newsstand, the flower cart, the shoe shine attendants. I frantically scan the rows of ticket windows. I haven't formulated the details of this mission, but it doesn't matter. Gert-Jan and the infant are nowhere in sight. I scan the dingy atrium once more, then sprint for the escalator. I hurdle the steps three at a time toward the departure gates.

I'm afraid I'll race into the waiting area only to witness the bus pulling away with Gert-Jan staring out the rear window with an expression of mystery and malevolence. But instead none of the scheduled buses have even arrived. Jaundiced lights buzz overhead. The edges of a color-coded transit map peel off the wall. The few waiting passengers keep to themselves. An elderly man with thick glasses secretively tugs chewed gum from beneath the wooden benches. As I stroll down the passageway, I remove my knife and release the blade.

At the far end of the corridor, Gert-Jan stands cradling the infant. I wipe my palms on my jeans and clench the knife handle tighter. There's nobody else for fifty yards. Gert-Jan gently rocks the blue blanket and sticks out his tongue at the newborn. He's so absorbed that he doesn't register my approach. I move several steps closer, but am halted by soft blissful coos. The baby affectionately dotes on Gert-Jan. A minuscule arm reaches from the swaddling to pat his nose like a comrade. The sight sends a spiraling chill through my entire body. Whatever my plan was, it falls apart right here.

I descend the escalator with heavy steps. I toss the knife into the nearest trash can. Overhead there's the familiar rumble of a bus entering the station, breaks squealing like a high-pitched siren. I picture Gert-Jan boarding the vehicle with his new pet and surveying the landscape as they're conveyed beyond the borders of the city. I should be relieved, but instead it feels like I've been abandoned.

There's a bar tucked away in the far corner of the station

and I find myself at the furrowed wooden counter. A shot of something sits in front of me. The bartender pays me no mind, mechanically cleaning glasses with a black towel. I see a small arm sticking out of my bag and unpack the doll that I had intended to give Ruth's baby. Despite its glass eyes and fixed antique expression, it bears an uncanny resemblance to the real infant. The smooth skin has an almost translucent sheen. The crinkled hands extend as if imploring to be held.

I lift the baby by one of its miniscule arms. It detaches with a soft snap that sounds like a sigh. The other limbs come apart just as easily. Several sharp turns are all that's required to unscrew the head. It's as if the poor creature was made to be dismembered.

I cradle the torso in my arms. It feels unspeakably vulnerable. I place my lips against the empty space where there used to be a neck. My voice whispers consoling words into that hole. There's only the faintest echo.

I END

When I reach the end of my history, I stop before etching the final phrase. I switch on the lamp on my desk and focus my eyes on the circle of light. I inhale a series of deep breaths until my pulse thrums in an unwavering rhythm and my hands remain perfectly steady. I'm about to perform a delicate operation.

I take the notebooks I've completed and methodically remove the pages. I slide each one beneath the aureole of light. Beginning with the last word I've written, I gently massage the letters away using a white eraser. I blow the rubbery residue from the paper and work my way backward, word by word, until I arrive at the beginning.

After the first phrase has been studiously scrubbed from the first page, I take a moment to admire my handiwork. The paper glistens with an otherworldly sheen. The ghostly traces that cling to these pages are my true story. I conclude my tale by inscribing the final line with the now sharpened point of my eraser.

CHAPTER 6
MY ZERO YEAR
(18 years old)

"The hunting dogs are playing in the courtyard,
but the hare will not escape them, no matter how fast
it may be flying already through the woods."
–Franz Kafka

LET'S PRETEND THE LANDSCAPE OUTSIDE THE BUS isn't familiar. At least for a little while longer. Through the dusky tinted glass, I imagine the scenery is nothing more than a film-strip of anonymous images. I pay no attention to the unevenly paved turnpike, the flower-choked median, the vista of rolling hills, the rows of religious billboards. The names of the approaching towns are just another collection of signs. I don't want to know how fast I'm closing in on my final destination.

As the scenery reels past the window, I focus on my reflection floating out over the yellow fields. I feel like a piece of thread being pulled forward by some unseen hand. The other passengers also seem lost in their own private dramas. Murmurs of distracted conversation. Half-remembered jokes and stunted anecdotes. People talking with their hands, carving incomprehensible patterns in the air. My seatmate switches on the radio and the sounds of a call-in show leak from his headphones. The shouted arguments are almost lulling. I lean my head against the windowpane, letting my skull vibrate along the same jittery frequency as the motor.

The cause of this trip is a letter. I had started to create a new life for myself when it tracked me down via registered mail. It arrived in a crimson envelope addressed in oversized letters to Jeff Jackson. Too intriguing not to open. On official legal stationery, a lawyer informed me that my mother was dead. He offered his sincere condolences concerning her sad and untimely passing. The letter stated I was her sole heir and included a bus

ticket so I could settle the estate in person. The lawyer empha-
sized the estate was significant. After several days convincing
myself I was more interested in the money than curious about
my mother, I boarded this Greyhound heading south.

When I step off the bus, the lawyer is there to meet me
at the station. He insists on being referred to as the "Estate
Disbursement Attorney," a term that so perfectly encapsulates
both his physical and spiritual dimensions that it might as well
be his given name. He drives us straight to the house where my
mother had been staying. As he navigates a series of bumpy
back roads, I'm relieved not to recognize anything. But the rows
of modest houses and neat lawns are soon replaced by stands
of pines, rangy shrubs, empty lots. The sky is steadily darkened
by green clouds of leaves. We're heading into the woods. As we
travel under the crosshatched canopy of trees, there's a shudder
of terrible recognition. When we turn off the asphalt lane and
pull into the winding dirt driveway, there's no longer any doubt:
This is the house.

It's a modest cottage with quaint wooden shutters. The place
has been spruced up since we lived here. The flowerboxes burst
with geraniums. A pile of stones have been used to start block-
ing out a garden. Someone has applied a fresh coat of yellow
paint to the walls and smartly etched the trim. But none of that
camouflages the fact this is the first house my mother and I
shared together. My first so-called home after an endless series
of orphanages and foster nightmares. Our first attempt at being
a so-called family. We lasted here about nine months, I think. A
small eternity by the calendar of our relationship.

The Estate Disbursement Attorney unlocks the front door
to let us inside. The sharp chemical smell is new, but the layout
of the rooms and even the severe angle of the afternoon light
in certain rooms are exactly how I remember them. These were
the sites of our first tentative encounters and occasionally suc-
cessful attempts to bond with one another. When I was sick, she

stayed up one night holding compresses against my fluttering chest. She taught me to read, patiently sounding out syllables and letter combinations. I recited the words back to her, imitating her own halting pauses.

But this isn't a lost Eden or anything. It was also the place where my mother first exhibited her savage temper. At any moment, the house could transform itself into a showcase for her binge drinking and sudden blackouts. She devised scarring punishments with oven burners, space heaters, and curling irons. But it was painful when she abandoned me, just the same.

As I survey the sparsely furnished rooms, unanswered questions about the house begin to nag at me. My mother had always been nomadic, ceaselessly shifting from one part of the country to another, rarely staying anywhere long enough for dust to collect behind the refrigerator. So I can't figure why she bothered to return here. Perhaps it was a simple decision of convenience, something close to coincidence.

There's a strained silence in the room. The Estate Disbursement Attorney clears his throat. In a hesitant voice that sounds like crumpling receipts, he says: "If you're curious, I'd be happy to tell you how your mother passed on."

His statement is so far outside my realm of caring that it takes me a moment to realize he's expecting a response. "Of course," I say. "How did she die?"

"Cancer."

The significance of the word is slow to register. This means she knew the end was coming. Her return to the house must have been purposeful. A gesture of sorts.

"Do you know why she rented this place?" I ask.

"Rent?" The Estate Disbursement Attorney shakes his head vigorously. "She bought the house. There's not even a mortgage. She owns it outright."

This news leaves me dumbstruck. It's difficult to process the fact that she would own any home. That she chose to buy this particular house is beyond the pale. Is it possible she nurtured a sentimental attachment to the time we spent here together?

The Estate Disbursement Attorney leads me into the kitchen. Atop a cheap formica table, my mother's ashes sit in a bright silver urn. After unpacking a stack of collated papers from his briefcase, the Attorney shares some preliminary details about my mother's estate. "There was no funeral," he says. "Instead, she's presented her heir with a formal series of last wishes." He picks up the first page of her instructions, scrupulously wipes his glasses on his tie, and begins to read.

First: She wants me to dispose of her ashes in a ceremonial fashion. I'm to follow the local river up into the mountains and sprinkle her remains at its source during sunset.

Second: She wants me to read a specific eulogy while I scatter the ashes. A notebook is provided that contains a lengthy existential reflection. She claims this ritual will be a healing ceremony to provide closure with the past. To break the circle, or start a new one, or some other predictable metaphor.

Third: She wants me to have this house. The deed to the property will be turned over to me, provided I carry out her last wishes and sign a legally binding document stating I'll make this my sole residence. If I agree, she expects me to move in immediately. There's not even the smallest hint about the place's possible significance to either of us.

"You either live here or you lose it," the Attorney emphasizes. "If you don't sign the form, the house goes to another relative."

My mother's will concludes with several brief lines about love. At first, I assume these are included out of deference to the conventional emotions that mothers are reported to feel for their offspring. But the awkward and halting phrases have a disturbingly genuine ring. They aren't much, but they're more than she uttered while she was alive.

The Estate Disbursement Attorney produces a copy of the residency document that I have to sign if I want to keep the house. I push it aside. It's too overwhelming to contemplate. "You've got a week to decide," he says. "I'll leave the form with you." Before he departs, the Attorney also hands over an official copy of the will, the notebook with the eulogy, and the silver urn full of ashes.

Once I'm alone, I wander through the house in a daze. I try to examine the place with an objective eye. Maybe it isn't so bad. The construction appears sturdy, the rooms are spacious, the southern windows offer scenic views of the surrounding woods. Even the weathered pieces of leftover furniture—the queen-size bed, the leather recliner, the expansive sectional sofa—seem comfortable. After all these years, it would be nice to have a place to call my own.

The walls are bare and the rooms scrubbed of personality, but a few of my mother's possessions have been salvaged. As soon as I pry open the cupboards and closets, they start to spill out. In the master bedroom, piles of neatly folded sweaters and faded dresses. In the foyer, a stash of yellowed paperback romances. Best of all, under the bathroom sink, rows of oversized plastic jugs filled with gin and vodka. An unsurprising stockpile.

I investigate the guest bedroom. In the far corner of the closet, a series of cardboard boxes have been stacked. I'm startled to find them brimming with bits of my childhood. I place each piece on the floor, like an archeologist separating the various strata and undertaking a careful inventory. There are a few scraps of clothes. Ancient T-shirts, mostly. A series of drawings hail from different eras. Many are pure splotches of exploded color. A few resemble splayed and dissected bodies.

The last box dates from the time just before I ran away. A tattered school text about the civil war, a mangy baseball cap, and one of my treasured cassettes. I used to make mixes for myself by taping favorite songs off the radio. The black ink has paled, but I can still decipher the song titles scratched across the plastic case. I thought I'd brought all these tapes with me, but I must have orphaned this one.

I uncover a cache of equipment in the hall closet. From an ungainly heap of clocks and lamps, I extract an old boom box. At first, I hesitate to set up the machine and insert the cassette. My finger presses play with a mixture of dread and anticipation. I watch the black tape wind a precarious path through the spools. The music has a slightly warped warble, but the sound comes through clear enough.

I recognize the songs immediately, but something about them has changed. The tunes have fermented and soured. Instead of remembering the solace they brought me, the music hurtles me back to the desperate time when I taped them. It's as if the sadness of that younger person has leeched into the very fibers of the magnetic tape. I start to feel lightheaded. It's hard to breathe. By the third song, I've fled the room.

After a few minutes pacing the garden, I regain my composure. I scoop up a stone from the nearby pile and return to the house. I unplug the boom box and tip it gently onto its side. Then I attack the machine. I strike it with the stone over and over, harder each time, thrashing it with a reckless fury. I smack it until the plastic cracks, the interlocking gears fracture, the metal innards break apart. I smash each of the pieces into still smaller parts. Plastic splinters spray everywhere until the machine is dispersed to a fine scattering of faceless trash. Until it's finally something I can bear to look at.

I've earned a bottle of vodka. I slump onto the living room floor and take a serious swallow. The burn could never be strong enough. I ease onto the living room floor opposite the urn, as if we're engaged in a staring contest. I open my mother's notebook and flip through the pages of her elegy, hoping they'll offer some insights. But there's only empty platitudes about rituals neither of us understand.

I keep drinking to dilute the floodtide of memories about the times my mother did X, Y, and Z. Soon I'm so blind drunk that I can barely stand. The walls feel like they're contracting around me. The sunlight filtering through the windows shrinks until it's nothing more than a spotlight at the center of the room. This house is my mother's trump. Her way of staking a claim on me. Exerting an influence in death that she couldn't in life. I'm a child again, buried alive in the same hole. I've boomeranged back to the beginning.

There has to be some way to break her spell. I drink my way through the upper part of a bottle of gin, then careen into the kitchen carrying her ashes. With a dramatic flourish, I dump the silver urn at the bottom of the trash can. I throw back my head in defiant laughter, but the sound is a pinched whinny trapped in my throat. Maybe an hour later, I find myself digging the urn out of the trash. I return the canister to its position opposite me.

A few glasses later, I stumble out of the house with the urn tucked under my arm. I head into the woods. It's a relief to be outside and there's a lightness to my unsteady steps. But as I travel further, an eerie familiarity settles over the sights. The feathery quality of light filtering through the branches. The purposeful arrangement of gigantic boulders under a lightening-struck oak. The trickling water patterns of the creek at low rainfall. In a lonely place in the forest, I begin to dig a hole.

I scoop out the raw reddish earth using my hands. Dirt smears my forearms. Fibrous roots collect under my nails. I place the urn in the rutted ground and cover it with mud, twigs, and pine straw. I stamp down the grave until it blends seamlessly with its surroundings. Once I figure that I've camouflaged the spot well enough that I'll never be able to find it again, I weave my way back to the house. I crack open a fresh celebratory jug of something or other.

It's probably morning when I find myself weeping in the middle in the woods. I'm bent over, hands clutching my knees, sobbing hot tears. A beard of snot covers my chin. I stagger through the forest, my feet wandering about somewhere beneath me. Every few steps, I tumble to the ground. Finally it's easier to crawl on my hands and knees. I'm convinced I'll never be able to locate my mother's ashes, but the awkward mound of earth is easily spotted even by my bleary eyes. I plunge my hands into the hole and with surprisingly little effort pull out the silver urn.

Back at the house, I puke in the kitchen sink. I heave up watery mouthfuls of undigested alcohol and sticky plumes of black-green mucus. My throat is red and blistery. I collapse on the floor and lie half-conscious next to the dirt-encrusted urn. The seal has broken and some ashes spill out. They're nothing more than sooty snowflakes. Maybe I've been uncharitable toward my mother, incapable of seeing the house as an olive branch from beyond the grave, a gesture of forgiveness, a gift. I try to absorb some vibration through the urn's metal casing. I keep turning it over in my hands, hoping the right angle will release a signal from my mother, the way sea shells contain the sound of the ocean. Soon the exterior of the canister is covered with fingerprints, its shiny surface blotted out by my own greasy whorls.

I wake up staring at the floorboards. The air is scented with stale sweat and sour alcohol. There's a dull plaque of vomit on my tongue. I'm slow to notice the cold evening light that leaks through the windows. The front door is open and the wind escorts a party of leaves across the carpet. A circus of white moths circle the lamps. I try to decipher the faint noises that seem to be calling from the forest. It's probably just the insistent whine of the wind. But it also sounds similar to the baying of a distant pack of dogs.

Lying here, I'm overcome by a surpassing sense of peace. In a rare moment of clarity, I know what I have to do.

First: I flush my mother's ashes down the toilet.

Second: I tear up the letter of residency and toss it in the trash can.

Third: I rip the pages of the eulogy from the notebook, add them to the trash, and incinerate the whole lot.

I watch my mother's last wishes curl in the fire until I'm positive there's nothing left to salvage. Until they're nothing more than a fistful of cinders. My attention turns to the half-empty notebook. I stare intently at the remaining blank pages. They seem to beckon. Slowly I screw up my courage. I want to write some version of what's happened to me, but I have no idea what sort of story might spill out. I place the notebook on a flat surface and fold it open to the third page. I tap my pen against the paper. One, two, three. It's time to begin.

MIRA CORPORA

(My first fiction)

"Passing off what might be true as fiction seems
a better vocation to me than passing off what is
quite possibly fiction as truth."
—Robert Frank

IT BEGINS WITH A TREE IN A FIELD. A LONE
orange tree in the middle of a grassy field. Observe how the moon
shines exactly three-quarters bright. A warm scentless breeze tick-
les the undersides of the shiny leaves and orbs of fruit can be seen
glistening on the branches. Plenty of ripe oranges for the taking.
This scene resembles something out of a painting, the ethereal daubs
of blue moonlight, the robust sinews of shadow, the perspective so
flat as to be unreal—and then it is a painting, tacked in a gilt
frame, perfectly centered on a white wall, hanging inside a gallery. It
is still night, the building is dark, and nobody is there to watch it.

A guard enters the room. His flashlight beam frisks the walls
and corners of the back gallery. He could've sworn he sensed the
hum of another presence. Someone staring at this painting. He
checks the locks on the windows, inspects the pipes crisscrossing the
ceiling, opens the recessed janitorial closet to study the assortment
of frayed mops. His eyes rove the opposite wall and inevitably stall
on the canvas of the orange tree. A mundane image, but if you
look long enough the still-life starts to pulse with a sense of longing.
The mysterious combination of pigments casually suggests not an
idealized vista in this world but an imperfect pane into another. Of
course maybe he's just been on the job too long. That's what happens
when the only company is the ringing thump of your own footsteps.

The shift is almost over. Ralton arrives to replace him and they bullshit for several minutes about the college baseball playoffs. Then the guard gets in his car and drives through the few white-washed blocks that constitute downtown, past the flickering gas lamps and sleeping boutiques, toward the old highway. The usual routine. But he can't shake the feeling that something is slightly off. His forearm lolls out the window while the truck bounces along the two-lane asphalt strip. The oil derricks loom out there in the darkness, a hot salty breeze carrying the creak of their repeating gyrations. The secret theme song of this vast nowhere. Tonight a watery red glow emanates from the scrub fields. Some kind of repair job, probably. Men with acetylene torches laboring under klieg lights. The guard thinks about his cousin who occasionally works on those massive steel structures and wonders what sort of life it might be. But enough of that. The truck turns into a half-vacant parking lot. The cantina calls.

The smoky room is lit solely with strands of blinking red and green lights, but it's easy to spot Malcolm and Blundell at the bar. They're the only gringos here. The guard strolls past a table of brooding Mexicans in cowboy hats and takes his customary stool next to Blundell. He orders a shot of whiskey as a doleful ranchero blares from the jukebox. Malcolm fills him in on the baseball game, the local kid who struck out with the bases loaded in the bottom of the seventh then botched a double play the next inning. The guard lets out a bitter laugh, relieved not to have money riding on the outcome. They both wait for Blundell to chime in, but he seems strangely preoccupied. He ruts his fingers through his tight blond curls and keeps his eyes offhandedly pinned to the entrance.

When the skinny shadows of the skaters materialize at the back door, Blundell hops off his bar stool and breaks into a sloppy grin. He tries to play it cool as the boys greet him with a series of rhythmic palm slaps and finger snaps. These surly brats have been hanging round Blundell for weeks now. They're probably just his errand boys in a small-time empire of pastel pills and powder-filled packets, but something about their interaction makes him uneasy. It's the way Blundell continually taps their elbows like a third base coach, the earnestly disinterested tone he adopts when talking to them, the conspiratorial smiles he flashes when he assumes nobody's watching. There's a feeling here the guard isn't ready to name.

The skaters sidle up to the bar. They jackknife their boards into the brass foot rail and strike low-wattage poses meant to signify a contempt not worth fully embodying. Several wear old Halloween masks perched atop their heads. Sometimes the guard forgets the skaters are so much younger than him. The little monsters act like they inhabit an alternate universe. Malcolm tries to make small talk about the ball game but the skaters just snigger, none of them having any fucking idea what he's gibbering about. Blundell attempts to smooth things over by ordering them a round of drinks, but they only cackle harder. The blue-haired skater sneers that the thrill of underage alcohol consumption faded years ago and besides they've got a better buzz stashed behind the dumpsters. An awkward silence as the jukebox drops a needle on a sorrowful salsa number. For the first time, the guard notices a fresh face among the usual gallery of sullen stares: A pale boy with stringy black hair and sunken spaniel eyes who holds himself a few paces from the others.

Blundell announces there is business to transact and squeezes into an empty booth with the skaters. The boy stands behind them without joining the conversation, executing an awkward pose that flits between involvement and invisibility. The guard thinks the boy must be younger than the other skaters, his ripped jeans and ratty green sweater more genuinely haphazard than their expertly studied ragtag fashions. A runaway, maybe. Malcolm has seen enough and stomps out the exit without so much as a wave. The guard remains at the bar for several minutes, counting the colorful rows of liquor labels and humming along to the listless static of the television set. He's contemplating leaving when the boy eases onto the stool beside him and asks him to order him a beer.

Hard to tell if this is some brand of provocation. The boy downs several swallows of alcohol before meeting the guard's gaze. Hints of rough experience are etched in the margins of his smooth features but there's also an unripe quality. The look of someone on a long trek who hasn't traveled very far. The boy finishes his beer and peers over his shoulder. "Can I tell you a secret?" he asks. He arches his eyeballs meaningfully in the direction of the booth of skaters. "Your friend is in love with the blue-haired one," he says. This is a dizzying thought and the guard doesn't know how to respond. "That isn't like him at all," the guard murmurs. Before he can say anything else, Blundell and the gang of skaters walk toward the bathroom and disappear inside together. "But that wasn't the secret," the boy says. "The secret is they're going to kill him."

The guard orders another round. He's not sure what else to do. It's as if he's been living inside a two-dimensional set whose walls have toppled, allowing him to survey the sprawling landscape for the first time. He feels lost. Maybe the boy is experiencing some-thing similar. Maybe that's why this peculiar child chose to confide in him so suddenly. There's something simpatico about the way the boy's hair shyly obscures his large eyes and the nervous way his fingers adjust the necklace of shells that encircles his delicate throat. The guard starts to ask about the skaters' motives and timetable, but instead he says: "Why are you hanging with those assholes?"

The boy contemplates his beer, as if trying to divine an answer in the bottom of the glass. He says: "Everyone needs a place to crash." The guard says: "My cousin has a spare room." The boy looks surprised by the invitation and suddenly the guard isn't sure why he made it. But then the boy says: "That could be okay." They both let their sentences trail into the air, the better part of the conversation remaining unspoken and partially obscured, like crossword blanks waiting to be filled in.

The skaters reappear from the bathroom. They scope the cantina to see if they're collecting suspicious looks, but the Mexicans remain indifferent. Blundell announces he's departing with the teens. He barely manages to suppress the self-satisfied smirk that twitches across his lips. The guard stares at his friend, surprised to realize that he isn't the least concerned about his safety. The threat is almost definitely overblown and besides the night's revelations have suggested a new realm where everything is permitted, or possible, or something. The blue-haired skater locks eyes with the boy and jerks his head in the direction of the exit. "We're going to check out this band at the Roxy," he says. But the boy remains slouched on the bar stool in a way that indicates precisely nothing. He twirls his thumb at the guard. "I'm crashing with his cousin tonight," he says.

The guard and the boy stand in the parking lot, under the trebly shadow of the flickering cantina sign, and watch the others depart. A warm breeze blows across the grease-stained expanse of gravel, inflating the skaters' loose shirts and whipping their long hair. They crouch behind the overflowing dumpsters and return cradling a rumpled paper-bag package so obviously illegal it resembles a decoy or prop. Several skaters pull on their birdlike masks with feathers and sequins. Blundell rolls down the window of his sedan and winks at his friend. Whatever that means. As the guard *watches the taillights seep into the darkness, he feels unaccountably giddy. The stars overhead seem scrambled into new constellations, suggesting a fresh zodiac. Casper Major, Galactica Minor, Vulcan Borealis. He idly wonders if he has just witnessed the last annoyingly cryptic gesture Blundell will ever make.*

"So," the boy asks, "where are we going?"

The guard remembers the red haze in the fields behind them. It's the answer that's been awaiting him. They set off together into the scrub brush, stepping gingerly across the uneven terrain, navigating a makeshift path through the skeletal bushes, the midget cacti, the thorns and burrs that tug at their pant legs. "We'll get the key from my cousin," the guard says. "He's repairing one of the derricks tonight." It might even be true. The itchy rhythm of cicadas sharpening their forelegs meshes with the propulsive whine of the oil rigs. It beckons them forward like a siren's song. "This isn't like me," the guard says, as much to hear the words aloud as for the boy's benefit. "I mean, I don't usually help strangers." The boy nods. He nervously plucks the pilings off his green sweater. Neither of them mentions Blundell or the skaters.

They step over a collapsed chain-link fence that marks some forgotten border. The flotsam of abandoned industrial equipment blankets the ground. Lengths of cast-off pipe, rusted lug bolts, tangled wires. The moon has been abducted behind a bank of grubby clouds and the entire landscape feels like it's been stripped to its shadows, chewed clean by the darkness. The boy scuffs his shoes against a shard of crushed boulder and struggles to keep his balance. The guard grabs hold of his hand—to steady him on his feet, of course—but then becomes self-conscious and drops it. The boy stares back at him with red eyes. The bleary crimson glare has hijacked the blackness of his pupils, giving him the endearing look

of a creature not quite human. "I've never been anywhere like this,"
he says. The unmissable undercurrent of naiveté strikes the guard
as almost heartbreaking.

They are getting closer. The guard can't help feeling like he's
traversing some extraterrestrial terrain. The red sun lies ahead and
tiny figures scurry beneath the silhouetted steel structures. The night
has been something of a puzzle but its overall contours are starting
to materialize in the guard's mind. He's picking up pieces on the
fly, amazed at how easily seemingly random events slot into their
proper places, suggesting a previously unknown pattern he simply
has to follow to its logical conclusion. Ahead of them a stand of
tall bushes rises from the otherwise arid landscape. Nobody can see
them here. The guard squats at the mouth of the grove and waits
for the next move to solidify in his mind. He sifts chunks of crystal-
lized sand through his fingers.

The boy clubs him in the head with a rusted pipe. The guard
flops to the ground clutching the back of his skull. His bloody lips
contort but no cries come out. He spasms like a piece of film caught
in the frame, an out-of-focus image that finally dissolves into still-
ness. The boy stares at the unconscious body. Smeared face-down in
the dirt, it no longer seems so menacing. The boy's cheeks are tear-
scorched and his entire being vibrates on some previously unknown
frequency. He seems unsure what business comes next. Eventually
he bends over the guard's softly panting form and removes his
leather wallet. He sweeps his index finger along the inner rim of
the billfold but doesn't bother to note the denominations or count
the credit cards.

The boy shambles into the grove of bushes with the stunted steps
of a sleepwalker. Short breaths wheeze in his chest. He realizes his
hand still clutches the lead pipe and he lets it drop. A dark sticky

substance coats his palms and he decides to assume it's the residue of rust. He wipes the salty sting from his eyes and pushes through the brambles. He stumbles upon a startling sight: A small stretch of oasis in the midst of all this desolation. He stands frozen on the edge of a patchy field. There is something tantalizingly unreal about this serene vista. Maybe it's a trick of the three-quarters moonlight, but the world around him appears unnaturally shallow, no more than a stretched piece of canvas. A reassuring thought, mostly. A lone orange tree stands framed in the middle of the field. A breeze tickles the undersides of the leaves and orbs of fruit can be seen glistening on the branches. They are ripe for the taking. But the boy has the uneasy sensation that if he reaches out to grab one, his hand will stab straight through the page.

NOTE ON THE COVER ARTIST

Michael Salerno is an Australian-born artist and filmmaker who lives and works in Paris. His work has been featured in numerous publications, on book and album covers, and has been exhibited in Europe, USA, and Australia. He also runs the press/label Kiddiepunk. You can visit his website here: www.michaelsalerno.net.

A QUESTIONABLE SHAPE
A NOVEL BY BENNETT SIMS

"[*A Questionable Shape*] is more than just a novel. It is literature. It is life."
—*The Millions*

"Presents the yang to the yin of Whitehead's *Zone One*, with chess games, a dinner invitation, and even a romantic excursion. Echoes of [Thomas] Bernhard's hammering circularity and [David Foster] Wallace's bright mind that can't stop making connections are both present. The point is where the mind goes, and, in that respect, Sims has his thematic territory down cold." —*The Daily Beast*

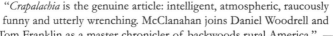

CRAPALACHIA
A NOVEL BY SCOTT MCCLANAHAN

"[McClanahan] aims to lasso the moon... He is not a writer of half-measures. The man has purpose. This is his symphony, every note designed to resonate, to linger." —*New York Times Book Review*

"*Crapalachia* is the genuine article: intelligent, atmospheric, raucously funny and utterly wrenching. McClanahan joins Daniel Woodrell and Tom Franklin as a master chronicler of backwoods rural America." —*The Washington Post*

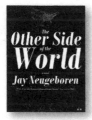

THE OTHER SIDE OF THE WORLD
A NOVEL BY JAY NEUGEBOREN

"Epic... *The Other Side of the World* can charm you with its grace, intelligence and scope... [An] inventive novel." —*The Washington Post*

"Neugeboren presents a meditation on life, love, art and family relationships that's reminiscent of the best of John Updike."
—*Kirkus Reviews*

SEVEN DAYS IN RIO
A NOVEL BY FRANCIS LEVY

"The funniest American novel since Sam Lipsyte's *The Ask*."
—*Village Voice*

"Like an erotic version of Luis Bunuel's *The Discreet Charm of the Bourgeoisie*."
—*The Cult*

FREQUENCIES

A new non-fiction journal of artful essays.

"The quality of each piece makes this journal heavy with literary weight."
—*NewPages*

VOLUME 1 / FALL 2012

Essays by Blake Butler, Joshua Cohen, Tracy Rose Keaton, Scott McClanahan; Interview with Anne Carson.

VOLUME 2 / SPRING 2013

Essays by Sara Finnerty, Roxane Gay, Alex Jung, Aaron Shulman, Kate Zambreno; A discussion about ghosts featuring Mark Z. Danielewski, Grace Krilanovich, Douglas Coupland, and others; Plus, T. S. Eliot interviews T. S. Eliot!

VOLUME 3 / FALL 2013, COMING SOON!

Essays by Lawrence Shainberg, D. Foy, Antonia Crane; and more!

HOW TO GET INTO THE TWIN PALMS
A NOVEL BY KAROLINA WACLAWIAK

"One of my favorite books this year." —*The Rumpus*

"Waclawiak's novel reinvents the immigration story."
—*New York Times Book Review*, Editors' Choice

RADIO IRIS
A NOVEL BY ANNE-MARIE KINNEY

"Kinney is a Southern California Camus." —*Los Angeles Magazine*

"[*Radio Iris*] has a dramatic otherworldly payoff that is unexpected and triumphant." —*New York Times Book Review*, Editors' Choice

THE PEOPLE WHO WATCHED HER PASS BY
A NOVEL BY SCOTT BRADFIELD

"Challenging [and] original... A billowy adventure of a book. In a book that supplies few answers, Bradfield's lavish eloquence is the presiding constant." —*New York Times Book Review*

I'M TRYING TO REACH YOU
A NOVEL BY BARBARA BROWNING

* *The Believer* Book Award Finalist.

"I think I love this book so much because it contains intimations of the potential of what books can be in the future, and also because it's hilarious." —Emily Gould, *BuzzFeed*

THE ORANGE EATS CREEPS
A NOVEL BY GRACE KRILANOVICH

* National Book Foundation 2010 '5 Under 35' Selection.
* *NPR* Best Books of 2010.
* *The Believer* Book Award Finalist.

"Krilanovich's work will make you believe that new ways of storytelling are still emerging from the margins." —*NPR*